Every Galaxy a Circle

Stories

Chloe N. Clark

JACKLEG PRESS

jacklegpress.org

Published by JackLeg Press, 2026.
© 2026 Chloe Clark. All rights reserved.
Printed in the United States of America.

ISBN: 978-1-956907292

Library of Congress Control Number: 2024945533

Cover design: Danika Isdahl

Praise

Chloe Clark is a master of blending the everyday with the strange, the supernatural, and the sublime. In *Every Galaxy A Circle*, she takes us far, far away, and brings us home again, whole yet changed.
—Christopher Barzak, author of *Wonders of the Invisible World*

Every Galaxy a Circle is a powerful, wide-ranging collection showcasing a vast array of possible worlds. The book feels like a cabinet of wonders, something greater than the sum of its parts, by its willingness to explore many genres and situations. It's in this generosity that the collection gains a lot of power—but more than that, the stories here have a ton of heart, telling the stories of ordinary people navigating extraordinary situations and finding out just as much about themselves as the world around them. This is really a book to get lost in and treasure.
—Anya Johanna DeNiro, author of *OKPsyche*

Ambitious and wide-ranging, *Every Galaxy a Circle* does what genre does best: explore the depths and outer edges of what it means to be human. Clark plays beautifully with time and transformation, longing and grief, questioning what we have now and what comes after. This is a rich and textured collection that haunts.
—Erika Swyler, author of *Light From Other Stars*

For my galaxy.

Contents

All of Your Others

The dachshunds had been given their baths. The house smelled of wet dog and the cherimoya blossom shampoo that she used on them. There were three dachshunds, and one of her, and so the baths took up a good portion of the day. After they had been allowed to run wildly around the house for a bit, she would take the brush to their coats. The dachshunds hated baths but loved to be brushed; they would have sat at her feet for hours as she worked the soft-bristled brush through their fur, if she ever wished to brush them for hours, that is.

She had found the brush, after a bit of haphazard searching, and was going to fetch one of the dachshunds when the doorbell rang. Everyone she knew always knocked. That's how she knew that it must be the representative. Her neighbor, Loretta, had said that the representative was a young man and that he had been exceptionally polite.

She sighed and answered the door. Outside was a boy, in his twenties and probably only just out of college, wearing a freshly pressed suit. She noticed his tie first, which was mauve colored with deep blue pinpricks of color scattered across it.

"Ms. Marie Helber?" he asked. He had a nice voice, pleasantly deep; it was the kind of voice that, years ago, Marie would have expected to come out of the radio.

"Indeed," she answered.

"I'm Eric, with the Lethe Initiative. We sent you a message a while back." He held out a card, which she ignored.

"Yes, I'm not interested. It's why I didn't respond." Behind her, the dachshunds had realized there was a Stranger at the door. They had begun to creep forward with grand plans of barkage.

"Well, ma'am, would it be alright if I came in and talked to you, anyway? We've been told we have to at least explain the process to everyone, even if they later choose to opt out." He slipped the card back into his pocket as he spoke and shifted his weight from one foot to the other. He reminded Marie of some of the children she had once volunteered with. The nervous way they had stood before her when they didn't know how to formulate the questions that they really wanted to ask.

"Alright, fine, come in." She decided there was no harm in being polite as long as she stood firm.

He stepped through the door, and each dachshund gave a single disappointed yap. They had hoped to chase him away with a chorus of barks at a slamming door. She led him to the kitchen. It was her favorite room in the house because the windows were huge and looked out onto the garden.

Eric sat down at the tiny kitchen table, and she asked him, "Coffee or tea?"

"Oh, coffee would be great! Thank you." He liked the old woman. There were so many he met who acted downright belligerent, even when they were eager to sign up for the initiative. He wondered, sometimes, if there was some kind of inborn antipathy towards the government. If there was a gene for it or something.

Marie was always careful in her coffee-making: two tablespoons of grounds, levelled off, per cup, and the water poured in a second after it boiled. She used one of the old-fashioned plastic cones with a cloth filter. She thought her coffee always tasted much better than any she could buy in a café.

"So, I'm sure that you've heard about Lethe." She nodded, and Eric continued, "We have almost 95 percent of the population signed on. Of course, it's done to children right away nowadays. Most adults do choose to use the chip as well."

"Cream or sugar?" she interrupted him.

"Just cream, please."

"Good, I'm the same way. Cream in coffee, sugar in tea, and never the twain shall mix." It had been a saying of her grandmother's, and she had found herself using it more and more as she got older. She wondered if folksy sayings were yet another side effect of aging. She set the mugs of coffee down and took a seat.

"Thank you," he said. "To continue, the initiative, over the course of its now ten-year history, has been a great success. It's saved billions in medical costs—fewer suicides, fewer cases of depression, a more productive workforce. It's truly incredible."

Marie looked out the window and noticed the sun hitting the grass. It reminded her of the glare off the water, of her sister all those years ago, swimming in the lake and yelling for Marie to jump in. "But, what about the side effects?"

He was surprised. "Side-effects? There haven't actually been any reported. It's a simple procedure, very safe. A hearing aid is probably more dangerous for you."

"I didn't mean physical side-effects. I meant mental ones, emotional ones."

He laughed. "No worries, ma'am! It helps you emotionally!"

"But you're losing something so vital, so intrinsic to who you are as a person," she said.

"Loss is vital?" He was confused.

"You're talking—your initiative is based on erasing memories. On removing my memories. How can that not affect a person?"

"You won't miss them. That's the point. You won't even know that you had them to begin with." He looked around the room, trying to come up with a helpful metaphor. His training officer had always stressed the power of a helpful metaphor. He looked at the dachshunds sleeping at her feet. "Like, let's say, there was a fourth dog out there that could have been yours, but it isn't, and you never knew that it could have been yours. Would you miss not having the fourth dog?"

Marie couldn't help smiling. The metaphor the boy used bordered on being so poor that it was almost poetic. She thought of her mother, who had taught introductory poetry to indifferent college students for years. Her mother said a metaphor worked best when it ended in a way that seemed impossible to predict but inevitable as soon as you heard it. "It removes them completely, though, right?"

Eric nodded, happy to have provided a way for her to grasp the concept of Lethe. "Any memory containing someone who has died will disappear from your mind. It will be like it has never been there. You might remember, say, going to Paris, but you wouldn't remember that you went with a girlfriend who has since died."

She thought of her father peeling apples at the table when she was young, how he always did it in one unbroken strip of skin. She asked, "How does one do that?"

"The process is painless," he said. He had been told to mention that as many times as needed. Marie looked back up at him, startled out of some thought. "And it's absolutely guaranteed. Even if someone came up to you and showed a picture of someone who had died, you'd have no recollection of them whatsoever."

She stared at him briefly and took a long sip of her coffee. "I bet you would, though. I bet you'd look at the picture and think you didn't know the person in it, but there'd be a—a something there. Like when you feel your stomach drop out in an elevator ride, and it's not as dramatic as when it does that on a rollercoaster ride, but it still gets to you, that whoosh feeling inside you. I bet there'd be something."

Eric's coffee was gone, and he fiddled with his spoon for a second, trying to think of a way to respond. "Well, isn't an unexplainable whoosh better than knowing you've lost someone?"

"Did you have it done?" she asked him.

He nodded. "Everyone who works for the government is required to get the chip upon hiring."

She nodded in response as if he had been the one asking a question. "Well, your coffee appears to be done, and I'm sure you have others you need to speak to today."

"I didn't convince you, then?" he asked.

"I'm afraid not. I'm just not willing to lose my loss, I guess."

He shook her hand, feeling a strange relief at not having swayed her. He wondered if one reached a certain age where memories were all that was left. He wondered what all the Lethed would do when they reached that age, and all their memoirs only featured themselves. She led him to the door, and he turned to her, fetching a card from his pocket. "I'm required, by law, to give you one in case you ever change your mind."

She took it from him, led him outside, and paused as she turned to close the door on him. "Do you have a big family, Eric?"

He was confused but answered. "Just my parents and me. I'm an only child."

She looked at him, weighing whether to say her next words, wondering what effect they could have on him, on his work. "Are you sure?"

She closed the door. She peered out the window and saw him standing on the doorstep, flustered, for a moment, before shaking his head and walking away. She got the brush and went to fetch the dachshunds. They were pleased to be getting the attention they were owed.

She thought about a boy she had once loved. He had died in a war. He had beautiful hands, like a detective in old black and white movies who always smoked cigarettes just so the camera had an excuse to linger on his fingers. She thought of her best friend. The size of her coffin and its overly shiny finish made it appear glowing under the church lights. She thought of her sister and her parents. There were so many people that one could lose in a single lifetime. The inevitable subtractions from one's life equation. There reached a point where the additions ceased. Maybe she was wrong. Maybe no one should have to live with so much death.

One of the dachshunds nudged her hand, prodding her to continue the brushing. She smiled and thought that she would probably miss the fourth dog.

Eric finished his rounds of visits for the day. Most people signed up in the end. He went home and made soup. He sat down to eat and thought of the old woman with the dogs. He thought of her question and felt a tickle in his sinuses like he did when he was trying to suppress a sneeze. It wasn't unpleasant, so much as like he was waiting for the sneeze, for something. He wondered, then, who they were, all of his lost.

The Rushing Waves

David's father had worked on submarines, far under the weight of the water, but he had always said that even in the deep there was light. Not light in the sense of actual light, but light in the way that he knew how water was filled with so much that was living. David thought that the same could not be said of space. The only thing in the Out seemed to be the absence of life, of light. He'd wanted so much to find beauty in that.

He never felt this way on the station. It was too large, too filled with the movement of people, to ever get lost in a moment of silence staring into the Out. Life on the station felt condensed to the next thing after the next thing. Just bodies with tasks to do, things to get done. When he had decided to work in space, he'd dreamed of how peaceful it would be, of being part of something infinite. But the reality was that it was mostly paperwork and research, the same everyday doldrums he'd have found in an office. At least it wasn't empty.

Why had he signed up for the mission, then? Maybe simply because he was one of the people who'd heard the distress call. The screams followed by silence and then something else—an eerie something that could only be described as close to singing, but not singing that any human had ever heard.

"David?" Katrine spoke from somewhere behind him. She was the mission's medical officer and someone whom David had never met before the mission's crew was introduced to one another. He sometimes questioned how, with a population of only a few hundred, he didn't know everyone on the space station by sight. It was smaller than a small town.

He turned away from the window. "Yeah?"

"You do that so often. What do you look for out there?" Katrine stepped closer, her eyes on the window, the darkness.

He shrugged. He had never really been looking out, just letting his mind wander in circles. "I think I'm mostly just staring into space."

Katrine laughed, and it took David a second to realize why what he had said was funny. "You know what they say, though, David, about staring into the abyss?"

David shook his head. He didn't know what they said, but Katrine had already turned to leave and didn't see his look of confusion.

David's father used to tell him about the sea. At night, David dreamed of the waves—of jellyfish, sharks, and squids with long tentacles. They weren't nightmares, though—not at first, not until his father never returned and David's mother moved them far inland.

David listened to the distress call again. It had started with a beacon—just the SOS code blipped out repeatedly from a ship called BNSi. The station control room eventually picked up the last message that had been sent out.

"Please, please, god. Please hurry." A woman's voice. When they had gone through the ship log data embedded in the distress call, it revealed that there were three female crew members; the voice could have been any of them. They'd each looked almost generic. One woman with shoulder-length blonde hair, two brunettes, all three looking at the camera with the exact same expression. The men had been the same. Maybe no one looks specific until you know them.

Then came the sound of screaming from somewhere behind the woman. Her voice had dropped to a whisper. "Please, please, please."

The "pleases" repeated into a mash of nonsense sounds. Then the singing. Or whatever it was. High-pitched and ethereal. It should have been beautiful, but the sound seemed to crawl from the speakers in the hush between screams. Cold and wet, it clung to David. He had the irrational thought that it wanted to curl up inside him and find a home for itself.

David wondered if the woman sending the message was still alive. What could have happened on the ship? A routine exploratory ship—BNS types were usually sent out from stations to do local recon and evaluation expeditions.

He pressed repeat, and the message played again.

"David, something's happened," his mother had said, shaking him from sleep with her hands on his shoulders.

He'd been dreaming of the sea, of shapes moving in the water. In a way, he awoke knowing something was about to change.

"Something with the sub. I don't know yet. They won't give me any information." His mother's voice shook, and she didn't take a breath between her sentences. It all sounded like one long, horrific word.

David thought of his father way down at the bottom of the sea. David stared at his mother, her eyes wild with fear, and he wanted to ask her to find a map and point out exactly where his father was. There was so much water. How did you find someone under all of it?

"We have visuals on BNSi," the mission captain, Andrew, announced. The crew sat around a small table. "Rescue mission protocol states that two of us must remain aboard our ship. That leaves four of us to embark on BNSi. Obviously, Katrine, as our medical officer, and I will be going aboard. Stacey, as our pilot, will be staying with our ship. Who else will go onboard?"

Darren, one of the other volunteers, raised his hand. David did as well, though, if he'd been asked, he'd never have been able to explain why. Just a flash of water across his vision, a shape. He could feel the other volunteer, Paula, relax in her seat beside him. It was one thing to volunteer for the mission, another to actually go aboard the ship where those sounds had come from.

"We'll prepare to board in T-minus sixty minutes. Be ready."

David walked back to the sleeping room. What had he just done? He could hear the singing in his head.

He looked at the window, into the Out. Such darkness coming in like waves. And then he saw it, floating in the black. The BNSi gleamed silvery white, looking so small amidst the Out. It was hard to think about what a speck everything was when encompassed by so much endlessness.

No one ever knew what exactly went wrong on the submarine. There had been survivors, an escape vessel of some sort that fit a couple of people inside. But the survivors all claimed some amnesia. It was possible, experts said, that the collective trauma had done something to their memories.

David's father was not one of the survivors.

There was no way to recover the body. What happened to a body enclosed in a submarine? Were the laws of decomposition the same? Or was it like a sort of stasis, and David's father was trapped in time, unchanging, until someone found him and set his body free?

David suited up. He watched the others, looking for the signs of nervousness in them that he felt in himself. Katrine slipped her helmet on, and he watched her face disappear beneath the visor.

"Are you ready, David?" she asked.

He nodded. "I think so. I've never done a rescue before. Have you?"

She shook her head. "Only in practice. Never in reality. I imagine that the practice was nothing like it actually will be."

"What do you think we'll find?"

Katrine faced him, but she may have had any expression under her visor. "Survivors, I hope."

The BNSi was silent. The main lights malfunctioned, flickering in and out in different shades of brightness. They all had flash beams equipped, but the steady lights did little to combat the dizzying effect of the flickering ones.

One of the doors was open, leading into the sleeping quarters. A man's body was on the floor. David stepped into the room, walking closer to the body. He heard Andrew say something, but didn't take in the words.

The man's face was turned to the wall. His mouth was open, and something leaked out—a silvery liquid that looked almost like mercury.

"Shit, there might be some sort of contaminant at work," Katrine said from beside him, having also stepped inside to look closer.

"It looks like his soul is coming out," David said. He hadn't meant to say it aloud.

The silver liquid formed a pool in the shape of a cloud. They both backed out of the room.

"I think we should be safe, since we're breathing through our masks, but I don't think we should carry anything back on our ship without a decontamination process," Katrine told the group.

"Have you seen something like this before?" Andrew asked.

Katrine shook her head, slowly, frowning as if considering something. "No, not exactly like this. No."

They walked on. Their footsteps, still the only sound on the ship. They had come to the control room. Someone sat at the computers. A woman, blonde hair pulled back in a sleek ponytail.

"Officer?" Andrew spoke.

The woman did not turn.

"Officer? We heard your distress call. We're here to help. Please acknowledge."

The woman did not turn. Katrine stepped forward, walking to the woman, and touched her on the shoulder. The woman fell from the chair like a ragdoll.

"Jesus fucking Christ!" Darren yelled, staring at the woman's now-revealed face. Her eyes were missing. It didn't look like they'd been removed, but rather as if they'd never existed in the first place—perfect, emptied shell-like spaces. Her expressionless face mirrored her crew photo. Silvery liquid glistened on her skin.

David was in his twenties when he found a survivor from his father's crew. Alyssa Harping. She'd been a medic aboard the submarine and didn't live that far from where he was going to university. They met at a café.

"David?" she asked when she saw him. She didn't look at anyone else, seeming to zero in on him though she'd never met him. He nodded, surprised. "You look a lot like your Dad."

"My mom says that too," he replied.

Alyssa sat across from him. "I don't remember anything about it. You've probably heard that about the survivors?"

"Yeah, but is there anything?" he asked.

Alyssa looked off into the distance; her response was a long time coming. "I can't say this is anything true or real. It's just something that I sometimes dream about."

She paused again, and he felt the need to prompt her. "Yes?"

"Sometimes I dream that I'm back down there, and there is something on the sub with us. A shadow where there should be no shadow. As if someone is standing there—but there isn't anyone standing there? I dream it so much that I wonder if it isn't some sort of memory, but what kind of memory could it be?"

"A shadow?"

"A shadow. That's all I have. I'm sorry, David. I wish there were more, but there's just an empty space where memories should be. It's like someone climbed into my head and scooped out everything. Your father was a good man. I'm sure whatever happened down there, he died being brave, helping someone."

They found most of the crew members. All in states of mysterious death, though none as bad as the eyeless woman. There was nothing to reveal what had happened. They downloaded the ship's data and prepared to disembark. Then a sound came. A sound like singing. The sound from the distress call.

"Where is it coming from?" Darren asked, looking around, terrified.

It seemed to be coming from everywhere at once.

Katrine went still. "It sounds like whale song, almost."

And it did, David realized. It sounded like a whale in distress, calling out through the oceans. Then the pitch went higher. And higher. It rang through his skull. He needed to block it out. The sound made his skull vibrate.

David used to dream of his father. Of his father standing on a beach at night, facing the ocean.

David would walk up to his father. "Dad?"

His father would turn to him. He was always smiling. "The water's so endless, David. Being a part of it is like being a part of eternity."

Then his father would walk into the ocean until he disappeared beneath the waves.

The singing stopped.

"We need to get out of here," Andrew said, speaking what all of them knew to be true.

They disembarked, leaving behind the bodies and the ship. They'd send a ship back, a ship equipped to deal with the decontamination. The bodies would not float in space forever.

David took off his suit and sat down on the ground, breathing in the safety of their own ship. His hands shook. He heard the song still in his head, ricocheting through his mind. Would he be able to hear it forever? Recall it, even, in his sleep?

It took three days to return to their station. David stared out the windows as they neared it. He was ready to see the safety of what he thought of as home. But the station was not there. Or it was not there as it had been. It was ruined, broken, destroyed.

Andrew sent a message in. No response. He sent a distress call out.

A voice came over the monitor. "Repeat, please. Did you say you're from Station Ellipto?"

"Yes, we're a rescue vessel. We were out on a mission. We're ship BNNi."

"Jesus, well you're one lucky damn rescue crew. Ellipto suffered a malfunction in one of the main ports of some sort. There was an explosion. We're listing no survivors. We didn't know there was a crew out. Do you have the resources to reach us? Or should we send someone to bring you in?" The voice was practical. Not even considering the emotional nature of the message they had just dispatched. Ellipto had been their home. Smaller than a small town.

"We…We have the resources to reach you," Andrew said, voice faltering.

Years later, back on Earth and working as a researcher for the stations, David found himself still dreaming often of BNSi. The vessel had never been recovered, lost in the mess of disaster. Researching it later, he'd been unable to find a ship with the name BNSi logged in any of the systems, and there was no way to notify the crew's families. He wondered if the mission was meant to have been out there at all.

Sometimes he still woke with the song playing in his head.

At an Oceanic museum, supervising a field trip for his daughter, he bumped into Katrine. She had aged so much. Had it only been a decade?

"David, how have you been?" she asked.

"Good, good. And yourself?"

"As fine as can be."

David's daughter looked at Katrine and said, "My grandfather went into the ocean, and my daddy went into space."

Katrine smiled. "I was in space, too. That's how I know your Daddy. Do you want to go into space or into the sea?"

His daughter thought for a moment. "The sea. I like whales."

"Whales are beautiful," Katrine replied.

His daughter nodded solemnly. "And they sing. Sometimes they sing warnings, you know. Of dangers in the deep."

A shadow passed over Katrine's face. "Yes, sometimes they do."

"But, you know, they also just sing sometimes. It's not only bad things they sing about."

David watched Katrine's face, wondering if she heard the song still, too.

"Is that so, dear?" she asked.

David's gaze drifted towards an aquarium. It glowed from some internal lighting that had been rigged up. He heard his daughter reply, "Oh, yes, they sometimes call out just to let each other know that there are strangers out in the deep. To not be afraid, because they aren't alone."

Cave Systems of the Midwest

In summer, when I was a kid, the dark was never really dark. I'd lie outside, the grass feeling cool beneath me, and stare at the sky, hoping to see bats. My mother would call me in eventually, one hand on her hip as she scanned the yard. She understood that I wouldn't come in until I'd seen at least one bat. Their bodies looked like the real night sky should, darker than dark, as they swooped overhead.

If I were honest, I'd say that I fell in love with my husband because of bats. We met when I was training to do a volunteer bat count. Darren was studying the spread of white-nose syndrome. When I think of the moment that completed Darren in my mind, it was the first time he had me hold a bat.

It was softer than I expected, the belly close to velvet in texture.

"Gentle," he said.

I had never held anything so delicately. "Now open your hands," he said.

And I did. And the bat flew off, rehabilitated and ready to go home. We watched it until it was just another part of the darkness, indistinguishable from the sky.

Three years later, Darren would be gone as well.

There was a memory of him that returned to me over and over, in my dreams, when I took showers, even when I walked down the street. He was leaning against the kitchen counter, drinking a glass of water, as I walked into the room. It was early in our relationship, and he'd woken up to get a drink, and then I'd woken up, forgotten he was there, and went to get my own drink. My heart jumped when I saw a person in the kitchen, but then he smiled at me as the streetlights flickered through the window onto his face.

It had been four years since Darren had left. Left, I said when people asked, because it raised no questions. It was funny how people felt it was improper to pick apart romantic disaster, but if I had told the truth, there wouldn't have been a problem. If I told someone it had been four years since Darren had disappeared, then they would probe me and ask as many questions as they could get away with. Being left was off-limits, but tragedy was fine to analyze.

After four years, I'd finally moved. A new place, with no past connections, felt right, felt needed. I had gotten a job at the police station, doing computer analysis work. There wasn't much of that, though, I'd learned quickly, and so mostly I seemed to be a very well-paid secretary. It could've been worse.

The walk to work, from my new apartment, was an easy one. Straight lines and half a mile. It was a small town trying to pass itself off as a small city. I'd heard from a neighbor that the town played up its quaint townness during the summer when tourists would swarm in. It had a lake at its center, along with national parks and camping grounds surrounding its edge.

The police station was tiny and looked like it belonged to a different time—red brick façade and hardwood floors on the inside. There was a single cell in the back, for keeping anyone who needed to sleep one off the sheriff had told me when he was giving me *the grand tour*, but most people just got driven to the county jail one town over.

"Good morning, Diana," the deputy, Arthur, said as I walked in.

"Morning, Arthur." I walked to the front desk and sat down behind it.

"You're in early, aren't you?" Arthur asked. He was sitting on the very corner of his desk, a pose I assumed he had gotten from some popular cop show about hard-living detectives.

I shrugged. Time had a funny place in my mind. I viewed it as taking me further and further from Darren, from some sense of closure. If I thought about it like that, then it became hard to keep track of specific hours.

"Oh, you know, still getting a feel for everything," I said because I couldn't really explain why I didn't pay attention to clocks. The phone rang. "Hello, Police, how may I help you?"

The calls were always simple things: strange vans spotted near the school that turned out to be parents, kids making noise, and even, once, an actual cat up a tree.

"It's my daughter. She's missing." A woman said, her voice not yet frantic but definitely headed down that path.

"Your daughter? For how long, ma'am?" I asked, trying to project calm across the phone lines.

"It's only been a few hours, but I think she went to the caves," the woman said. Her voice pitched higher at the word "caves," and it drilled down my ear.

I'm just going to the caves. I'll be back in a day. Those had been his last words. Not even words, just scrawled on a Post-It he'd placed on the fridge. A neon pink Post-It. It wasn't unusual. He was monitoring what he thought might have been a new kind of fungus. He'd been in and out of the caves for the past months. I didn't worry, threw away the note, made dinner for one.

I hadn't realized there were caves in this new place. Something I hadn't even considered. "The caves?"

Arthur looked over at me, a frown creasing across his face. He mouthed *caves* at me and I nodded back.

"The damn caves! I always tell her not to go near them!" The woman's voice was now at breaking point.

Arthur had scrawled out a note, and he held it up for me to see: *Tell her we'll send somebody out.*

"Ma'am, we're going to send someone out to the caves to look. If you could please give me your info so that I can give you a call back when the caves have been searched." The woman gave me her information, and I copied it down. I gave a few more reassuring words before hanging up.

Arthur was standing. "A kid in the caves again?"

I nodded. "She's been gone a few hours, her mother said. I didn't realize there was a cave system here."

"Quite an impressive one. Tourists used to poke around, but it gets dangerous very quick, so now it's closed up. Town over from us had a case of that white-fuzz because of the tourists, too, or whatever it was called?"

"White-Nose Syndrome," I respond automatically.

"That's it. Killed their whole bat population one year, 'cuz people from all over had been in and out. So that was another reason to close up our caves. Kids still find ways to get into the mouth. Gotta be mysterious, I suppose. They always get lost, though. I'll go check it out and see if I can find the girl." He grabbed his jacket off the back of his chair and headed out.

As the door closed, I was already sitting down and googling the caves. Not much came up, just a few stories over the years about people going missing and then being found. They were always found. I hovered over a link on the bat population but didn't click.

Hours passed, and I organized the filing system we were switching over to. When the door opened, and Arthur came back in, he looked exhausted.

"You find her?" I asked.

He nodded. "Yeah, she's at the hospital, getting a once over. Kid seemed real shook up."

"She just get lost?"

He shrugged. "Assuming so. I'm going to talk to her more tomorrow, when she's calmer. Make sure no one tricked her into going in. Sometimes kids do that as a joke. Jackasses."

At home, I looked up photos of the caves. It was still light out, wouldn't be dusk for another hour, so I drove out to look at them in person. Online, it said not much of the cave system there had been explored, that it was a dangerous one for the most part once you got past the wider mouth. Estimates were that it was only a few miles long. Over 400 miles of the Mammoth Cave in Kentucky had been explored. I wonder how long it took for someone to measure it out, to find the dimensions of its depth.

Parking in front of a beaten-down path towards the cave opening, I could see why Arthur had been exasperated. A few beer cans, some cigarette butts near the entrance, and the matted grass on the path, pointed to how many teens probably still used the cave as a place to hang out away from the gaze of adults. The opening had a haphazard chain in front of it, a single sign saying **Caution Keep Out**. It wouldn't have kept out so much as a lazy toddler.

The cave's mouth was about seven feet across, about eight feet tall. I imagined it got much lower very quickly if people had only explored the mouth without going further inward. Slightly dangerous and uncomfortable kept out tourists, but it didn't keep out cavers. I'd explored a few with Darren, though it had never really been my thing. I'd never seen the appeal of crawling on cold mud through the darkness. Though once, we'd crawled for about a mile and then suddenly been able to stand up. I thought I was imagining that it was brighter, but Darren had taken my hand and pulled me forward to where there was a hole in the roof, letting light pour in. On the ground, everywhere the sun hit, life grew. Plants, a single, solitary tree reaching upwards towards the light. In that moment, I thought I could have stayed there forever, in the quiet and the dark, with the one I loved.

I used the flashlight on my cellphone to peer inside the mouth; it was so dark inside. Cool air enveloped me as I leaned slightly past the entrance point. Sweeping the light around, I saw rock, some footprints imprinted into the ground, and then the girl. I nearly dropped the phone, as I gasped. A small girl stood at the far end of one of the walls, back pressed against the cave wall. She was covered in dirt. She saw me see her, and her eyes were so wide with fear. I took a step forward, and then my light went out. It should have been fine; the light from outside should have given me enough ambient lighting that I should've still been able to see the girl. But there was nothing, just pitch dark around me. The light framing behind me unable to penetrate anywhere else. "Hello?" I yelled out. But there was no answer. I reached my arms out, trying to see if I could find the cave wall, but there was nothing. Everything seemed bigger and further away. "Hey!"

Nothing. I stilled my breath and tried to listen for her breathing, using all the tips Darren had taught me to find my way. There was just silence. Soon, there was only the pounding of my own heart, like footsteps through forests crunching in my ears. I had to have imagined her. Some fear born out of memory. I stepped back into the light. The sun was setting, but shouldn't have been. I should still have time left. Back at my car, I checked the clock and over half an hour had passed. Did I stand there in the dark that long? My mind was playing me for a fool.

I'd never done vertical caving, but when Darren got into it, he would practice tying the necessary knots at night. We'd be watching a movie, or sitting in bed, and he'd knot and untie knot and untie next to me. One night, as he practiced a butterfly, I mentioned that he could do it easier.

"Easier?"

I motioned, and so he passed me his practice rope. I quickly looped it around my fingers, dipping the rope in and out fluidly. "Look, you can see the butterfly if you're doing it right." I cinched and passed it back to him.

"How'd you do that?"

"My dad used to take me out on his boat." I'd never forgotten the motions. My dad always said that a good knot could save a life.

Every time Darren did a cave dive after that, he'd tie a couple in front of me on his way out. Show me that he had learned them perfectly. It wasn't a vertical cave he was lost inside of. At least then, I could have blamed nature. The twists of weight and darkness. He was careful, fastidious, practiced always and everything. He should have been fine.

The next morning, Arthur asked me to accompany him to talk to the girl. "Listen, we don't have any women on staff but you, and honestly, I think she might be more comfortable."

22

She was still at the hospital. "Was she hurt?"

Arthur shook his head, "Don't think so. But she's really in shock, I guess."

She had her own room and was sitting in bed, staring out the window, when we walked in. She turned, and I almost lost my composure. But I had sat in police waiting rooms, had stared at phones waiting for them to ring for years, had sat through question after question. I knew how to contain an ocean. It was the same girl I had seen in the cave the night before. Small for her age, with a slightly heart-shaped face, and dishwater blonde hair that fell to her shoulders. She looked so sad and scared that it de-aged her from a teen to a child just woken from a nightmare, the moment before her parents came and turned on the light, when it was still just her and the dark.

"Hi," I said and stepped closer.

She didn't say anything.

Arthur said from slightly behind me, "Hi, Kara, we wanted to come check in on you. How you feeling today?"

She didn't say anything.

"Kara, hi, I'm Diana, I work with Detective Arthur at the police station," I said. I held out a hand, slowly, letting her relax to the sight of something moving toward her.

She took my hand, gingerly, and shook it.

"Hi, Diana." Her voice was barely above a whisper.

"How are you feeling today?"

She didn't answer, but started coughing hard. Her whole body shaking with the effort. She paused only to say, "Water, please?"

"I'll get it, gimme a sec," Arthur said and left the room. Kara stopped coughing immediately and gave me a look so determined, I imagined she would one day rule an army.

"I'm not supposed to be here," she said.

"The hospital?" I asked.

"No! Here! This isn't my home. The caves get so dark and so deep, and I got lost. I need to go home. I need to—"

"I—"

But before I could finish my sentence, Arthur was already back, a plastic cup of water clutched in his hand. He gave it to her, and she took a timid sip. "Thank you, sir."

"You're welcome. Now, we just wanted to ask you if you were in the caves for any reason?" I wasn't sure if I appreciated Arthur's directness.

She turned her face, not to Arthur but to me. Staring me in the eyes as she spoke, she said, "I lost something, and I needed to find it."

"Well, what did you lose?" he asked.

She shook her head. "I'm really tired, sir." She leaned back into her pillows, closing her eyes. Arthur motioned for me to follow him out.

"She's a weird duck, huh?" he said.

I nodded. "She seems pretty traumatized."

Arthur frowned. "Her parents came in to visit her yesterday after she was found. Her mom said *that's not my daughter.*"

"Her mom said that?"

"Shock does weird things to the brain, doesn't it? My brother died." I opened my mouth to express condolence, but he continued, "It was a whole lifetime back. And I remember when we got the news, my dad went out to the garage and began working on his car. It was eleven, maybe even twelve at night. And he started doing an oil change out there in the dark."

I remembered the third day when Darren hadn't returned. How every time the phone rang, I wouldn't pick it up. You'd think I would have jumped at the sound, ran to it for answers. But I didn't, I'd let it ring and ring until whoever it was would leave a message on the answering machine. I didn't want to talk to someone who might give me the news I didn't want.

Animals that evolve to live in caves are often blind and have other senses adapted to the dark. They are called troglobites, and their bodies are made for their environment; they'd find it hard to survive outside of it. Darren had said once that when he was a child, he had wondered what it was like to live in one cave for a lifetime, to be beholden to a universe the rest of us considered so contained and dark. But, as he grew older, he began to see how we all lived those lives. Every ocean and city and mountain, its own world.

If I had followed him into the cave, if I had let my body turn toward the dark, maybe over the years I would have come to understand it.

At home that night, I researched the cave system. They were believed to be Karst caves, limestone bedrock that dissolved away to form sinkholes and caves. I assumed that it was something that could be easily proved, but apparently, it had never been verified. Darren would have been able to explain the formation; he would have told me which bats would likely live there and what fungi might be growing inside its walls.

It likely took millions of years for the caves to form into what they are. Over the years, since the town was keeping track, at least a few dozen people have disappeared in the surrounding area. While most were found, there were a few cases where the person was believed to have died in the cave. One man had come out, but a few weeks later had been institutionalized. The dark does funny things to the mind, someone was quoted in the article.

Most of the local legends were the usual suspects: ghosts, and for a while, an attempt at creating a local monster—the Batroo— but it mostly seemed like the town and the cave stayed out of each other's business.

Hours passed as I read about the caves, and when my phone rang after ten, I almost jumped out of my skin.

"Hello?"

"Hey, Diana," it was Arthur, sounding exasperated. "I don't mean to bug you, but that girl. She apparently ditched the hospital and ran off. I was wondering if she said anything at all to you? When I was getting her that water? Just anything that might be helpful?"

I almost said something, and then stopped. I remembered the way she had stared into my eyes as if asking for help. "Not really. She just said something about being lost."

"Damn. Okay, thank you, Diana."

As soon as he hung up, I went to my car to drive to the caves, taking my storm flashlight and an old set of Darren's ropes with me this time.

The caves in the darkness looked less sinister somehow, the mouth just another shade of dark. At the closest tree, I looped around some rope, tying the knot tight. "See the wings," I whispered. The other side of the rope went through my belt loop.

I pressed the flashlight on and stepped inside. It stayed lit but only projected about a foot in front of me.

"Kara!" I yelled out into the black.

Silence.

I kept walking forward, the cave ceiling sloping further and further in until I had to crouch to go forward. After about ten minutes of slowly inching forward, my breath curling out of my lips in the beam of the flashlight, the first branch appeared. My first choice. I only had 80 meters of rope. It wouldn't take me far, wouldn't help me through too many choices.

"Kara!"

Silence.

I went left. The hand of my wedding band, never taken off.

In front of me, the tunnel was low, narrow. I got on my hands and knees, crawling forward slowly with the flashlight. I wondered if there were bats in the cave and imagined there were to keep myself company.

Bats are one of the best pollinators there are, just as important as birds and bees. Those daytime beauties, Darren would say with a roll of his eyes. The flowers pollinated by bats were usually lighter in color, pale shades, rather than the bright flowers of daytime pollinators. How many species would disappear without them?

Ahead of me, the tunnel opened back up. A slightly larger cave room, and took the chance to raise slightly and stretch out my knees. When had I grown aching and creaky?

"Kara!"

Silence. Maybe I'd been wrong. Maybe she'd stared into my eyes because there was nowhere else to look.

"Hello?" A small, trembling voice. I turned my flashlight to the sound, careful of sudden movements in a cave.

Kara was huddled against the wall of the cave.

"Hi, Kara, you remember me? Diana from the hospital?"

She shook her head. And I realized something about her was different. Her muddy jeans and pink shirt were the ones she went missing in, not whatever she would have been wearing when she ran away from the hospital.

"Kara, how long have you been in the cave?"

She started crying. "A couple days? I think? I got so lost, and all the other entrances opened out into places that weren't right."

"Okay, sweetie. Well, you're found now. You're going to get out of here."

I moved towards her, gently.

"Did you see me?" she asked.

"You?"

"There was a girl, me…she told me to stay put. She said she had to find her way home. But she was me." She was full-on sobbing now.

I peered around, three more cave tunnels in front of me. Three more branches of choice.

"Don't worry." I undid the rope from my belt and looped it through hers. Tied the knot tight. "You're gonna follow this rope back all the way to the entrance."

I handed her my flashlight. I took my phone out of my pocket. The screen was a picture of Darren standing in front of a cluster of bats flying out from under a bridge. He looked like joy. "You can call your parents, the phone will work as soon as you reach the entrance. It's not far at all."

She took the phone. "You're not coming. Are you looking for m—her?"

"I just need to see something."

"Okay." She gripped the rope and began to crawl alongside it. Before she dipped back into the tunnel, she turned back for a second and said, "Thank you."

"You're welcome."

"Not...not all the passages let you go back through."

I chose the left tunnel, again, before the light from the flashlight had faded completely. I crawled forward in the dark. The tunnel got tighter and lower. If I got stuck, there'd be no way out. I kept going forward, the tunnel tightening around me until I was struggling, pushing, pushing forward. It could have been an hour or ten minutes.

I could barely squeeze forward anymore. Is this what Darren did? Had he pushed and pushed, trying to get free? Had he yelled for help? He must have been so scared. He must have felt so small.

And then my hand hit a different kind of ground, smoother rock, wet. Not quite as cool as the ground beneath my body. I dug my fingers in and pulled with all my force. I could feel the earth giving away slightly, just enough around my body. And then I was pulling myself free into a larger chamber. I could feel fresh air. I crawled forward towards the air until I was crawling out into the woods. I lay on the pine needle-covered ground for a few moments, gasping for air. Up above, the stars shone through the trees, but the sun was already starting to rise. How long had I been in the cave? I pulled myself up. These weren't the woods I recognized from around town, but it still felt familiar. I looked around at the pines, the lichen on oak. I knew these woods.

I stood, legs shaking from the exertion. I could hear a road not too far away. I ran towards it. A few cars making an early commute. I knew this road, had driven it a thousand times. I began to jog towards town.

It wasn't far. A twenty-minute run and I could see my house. The flower garden out front, filled with pale blooms. The key under a statue of a salamander. I opened the door and stepped inside. It was so quiet, I couldn't bear to break the silence by calling out and not getting an answer. I walked to the kitchen. The red-pink light of the rising sun bled across the room. But the kitchen was empty. I leaned against the counter, let the world catch up to me. My whole body shook.

"Hey," Darren said from behind me in the doorway. "Where have you been? I was beginning to worry."

Outside, I saw a bat swooping downwards, racing against the light of the sun.

Leopard Seals

There was always something in the water whenever Karynn dreamed of the sea. The dreams changed often—sometimes she was in a boat, swimming, cast out on an ice floe—but always, always there would be a shape under the waves coming for her. She'd wake every time, before it reached her, and for some reason, that terrified her more. It was always coming for her without ever catching her, and so there could be no escape. There was no way to survive something that hadn't happened yet.

She moved for a job, the same year that she turned twenty-five, to the biggest city she had ever lived in. A friend of a friend was letting her apartment sit for them while she looked for a place of her own. The apartment was lovely—spacious and old—she had never imagined living, even temporarily, in such an elegant space. The one thing that caused her pause was that it was run by a board of tenants; the person who she was sitting for told her that there was a list of rules to mind. "Remember the rules," he had told her more than once.

Karynn tried to make herself fit into the living space of another life. It was easier than she expected. She hadn't brought much with her, waiting for her own place before she had all of her things shipped, and what she had was easy to stuff into a couple of storage containers. She pulled out blouses and, for once, was pleased that her clothing wasn't so expensive that it needed to be hung up. She liked going off to work feeling as if her life was finally on a good course. She liked imagining that she was the kind of person who could live in an elegant apartment and wear nicely coordinated outfits.

The invitation came on a Wednesday, pushed under her door. It was on elegant cream-colored cardstock and written in fountain pen. Karynn was invited to a floor party at Apartment 717. She wondered if it was meant for her or for the actual owner of the apartment at first, until she saw her name stenciled in gold foil on the back of the card. Her name seemed prettier somehow when she saw it like that—the name of someone in a romance novel or a fairy tale. She went to tuck the invitation somewhere that she would remember it and noticed that it smelled slightly of roses and vanilla—not the manufactured scents but rather as if it had been rubbed in rose petals and lightly spritzed with pure Madagascar vanilla. She held it up to her nose, closed her eyes, breathed in deeply, and imagined the person who would go to all of that trouble for a simple floor party invitation. She imagined a woman dressed in a silk dress covered in flowers and vines, a woman with long fingernails painted the color of the inside of oyster shells, a woman with perfect makeup that accentuated every sharp curve of the skull beneath her face, a woman whose eyes looked like a deep blue until you leaned closer and closer and they turned darker and narrowed and the pupils expanded until the eyes were black. Karynn snapped her own eyes open, shaking the image from her head.

The party was to be on Saturday. Karynn hadn't really met anyone in the apartments yet, so she figured that she should go.

...

Music came from under the door of apartment 717. It was a soft something—it had lyrics but in a language that Karynn didn't recognize, and the melody seemed not quite pop but not quite any other genre either. She knocked on the door twice.

A man opened the door. He was tall and youngish, maybe mid-to-late thirties, and dressed in a way Karynn could only have described as chic casual. She hated herself a little as she thought of the description, but there it was.

"You are?" he asked. He had a pleasant voice, with a light accent, from somewhere British.

"Karynn. I'm apartment sitting, two floors down," she replied. Nervous suddenly. She wondered if, maybe, the invitation was a mistake.

"Oh, of course, our newest building member. Come in!" he said. He swung the door open wider, ushering Karynn inside. There were twenty or so people milling about inside the apartment, which was lavishly furnished. The carpeting was plush beneath her shoes, and she wondered how it would feel against bare feet, maybe like walking on whipped cream. "I'm Laurence, by the way. I live across the hall."

"It's nice to meet you," she said. She couldn't stop her gaze from wandering around the apartment. The couch was one she had seen in a style magazine; it cost several thousand dollars. The bookshelves looked like they had been hand-carved out of the trunk of some massive tree.

Karynn's gaze landed on a woman across the room. She was the most beautiful woman Karynn had ever seen: tall and lithe. Karynn had never used that word to describe someone's appearance before, but it was the first word that came to her mind, lithe rhymes with scythe, she thought to herself. The woman wore a light blue dress. It was made of silk, or some fabric like that, and seemed to wrap itself around the woman. Not just in that it fit her form perfectly, but that it seemed to move with the shape of her body as she turned to stare back at Karynn. She smiled. She had a perfectly even set of white teeth, and her mouth was wide without upsetting the proportions of her face. Karynn had once read that beauty could be most easily identified by the proportions of a person's face. The evenness of each feature's alignment. The woman looked like her face was two sides of a mirror. She began to walk over towards Karynn and Laurence.

"Laurence, who is this?" she asked. Karynn tried not to jump in surprise. The woman had a distinctly unpleasant voice that seemed wrong with such a beautiful appearance. Her voice was high-pitched and sharp.

"Karynn, she's the apartment sitter, two floors down," he said.

"Of course! I'm Marissa. The owner of this apartment and I sit on the board of tenants. I had to approve you as an apartment sitter, you know. Rules, rules." She accentuated the word "rules," rolling it off of her tongue like it was a taste she didn't want to let go of. She held out a hand, and Karynn shook it. Marissa's skin felt soft, not a single callus.

"Well, thank you for approving me! It's such a lovely building," Karynn said.

"That it is. Historic, you know. Just mind the rules. Our board can get a bit…irate, when people don't follow them to the T." Marissa smiled again, such white and even teeth.

Karynn nodded, "Of course. I'm a rule-follower. That's what people always say about me."

Karynn wondered at the words that sometimes came out of her mouth. When had she begun to sound so meek? Was there a point in her childhood when she had firmly decided that strength and rebellion were just not something she could ever aspire to? She tried to smile at Marissa and Laurence, trying to make it seem like she had been merely making a weak joke. They both, though, were nodding appreciatively at her words.

"If only everyone felt that way, dear," Marissa said. Someone else, a tall man in a dark suit, had walked up to her and tapped her on the shoulder. She spun away from Karynn and spoke to him in hushed tones. Laurence walked away to another group of people, without a second glance. Karynn turned, not wanting to appear like she was listening in. She overheard the words "number 27," though.

She saw a table with snacks laid out on it and walked there instead. The snacks, or *hors d'oeurves* as she corrected herself in her mind, were gorgeous looking: tiny cakes with intricately etched patterns in the frosting—tiny whirls and petite flowers that must have been piped on with some kind of special frosting tool. Miniature quiches and savory tarts were lined up in rows. She picked up a flute of wine and took a sip. It was chardonnay of some sort, crisp and sweet. Picking up one of the tiny cakes, she popped it into her mouth, feeling guilty eating something that wouldn't have looked out of place on display at a museum.

Someone walked up to her. She could tell, though her eyes were closed in savoring wonderment. She opened them, quickly, and was staring into the face of a guy who seemed roughly her age.

He smiled, "Karynn, right? You're house-sitting for Micah?"

She nodded, trying to place his face in case they had met at some point, and she should have remembered his name.

"I'm Davis. I live across the hall from him, well, from you right now." He extended a hand, and she shook it.

"Oh, are you in music or something?" she asked. She vaguely remembered talk of a Davis.

"Yeah, well, I'm not musically-able. But I do PR work for bands. And you have a job…"

"I'm working at Treyes and Merrick, the law firm."

"Oh, are you a paralegal?" he asked. It was the tenth time since moving to the city that she had been asked this.

"No. I'm a junior associate, actually," she said, apologetically.

"Wow, so you're a lawyer?" It came out between question and not-question.

She nodded. "I focus on contractual rights, mostly."

Karynn's parents had been surprised at the single-mindedness with which Karynn had kept a 3.9 GPA during college, graduated a year early, and then immediately applied to law schools. When she graduated from law school, she'd overheard her mother talking to her aunt. Her mother, in a tone of pure surprise, had said that she never thought Karynn had it in her. *A lawyer's assistant, sure, an accountant, definitely, but my Karynn, a lawyer. She'd have trouble arguing with people who told her her eyes were neon pink colored.*

"That's really great. Contracts are something no one ever seems to know anything about. The number of times I've had to work through one with a band is just, like, a huge number," Davis said.

"They can be tricky," Karynn said. She wondered how impolite it would be to shift slowly down the food table and away from Davis. There were mini-pies she could see at the end of the table, the farthest from her. They had little poofs of meringue on top, goldened just slightly.

"They really can. The language is often so weirdly combined. It's like, can these two words really be used together like this? And then they mean the exact opposite of what they should," Davis continued to talk. A young woman swooped in on them as he spoke. She was dressed in a mini pink dress and four-inch heels, decidedly out of place.

"Davis! Can we go yet?" she asked. She eyed up Karynn with a sideways glance. Karynn tried to figure out why the woman seemed familiar.

"Um, I think Marissa would be expecting us to stay at least an hour," he said. Karynn thought about seizing the opportunity and heading for the pies. "Karynn, this is Lucy."

Karynn sighed inwardly. "Hi."

"You live here?" Lucy asked. She had shifted her weight onto one foot, so that her opposite hip jutted out at an odd angle.

"I'm apartment sitting for someone. So I don't really live here, just sort of, I guess," Karynn said. She realized why she recognized Lucy. She was the lead singer in some up-and-coming indie band with a terrible name—Dilapidated Platypi, or something close to that.

"Oh, that's fabulous, apartment-sitting," Lucy said, her tone betraying that she couldn't think of anything more pedestrian than apartment-sitting.

"You know, I have to go, introduce myself to someone over there," Karynn said, pointing vaguely off at a small group of people. "See you both around."

Davis began to say something, but Karynn had already made her escape.

Karynn wandered over to the group of people she had pointed at. She had no intention of talking to them. Laurence appeared beside her.

"Enjoying the party?" he asked.

"The food, the *hors d'oeuvres,* are amazing," she said.

"Marissa does go all out. She calls in these caterers, from god knows where, who cost some ridiculous amount of money per hour. But goddamn, those little cakes."

Karynn smiled, a real smile. "Those cakes are insane."

"You should try the pies. I think I'd give up sex for those pies." Laurence said to her, his gaze though was across the room. She followed it to Davis and Lucy, who were having some sort of heated talk. "Have you met those two?"

"Yeah, Davis lives across from me."

"That Lucy, does too now. She is a something," he said.

"A something?" Karynn asked.

"A something," Laurence repeated. "Sorry, that sounds rude. I'm just not a huge fan. I live directly on the floor above them. Very loud fights and other things."

"Oh," Karynn said. Unsure if she should, or wanted to, ask any questions or encourage Laurence on.

"I actually just complained. I feel….bad for doing so. But there are rules about noise." Laurence shrugged as if doing so absolved him of feeling guilty about complaining. He had broad shoulders, Karynn noticed. "Well, I should let you enjoy the rest of the party."

He walked off before she could respond. She didn't stay at the party long. She met a few more people from the building. They all had names that were easy to forget, and so she hoped not to ever be stuck on the elevators with them in the future.

Karynn dreamt that night of floating in the water. The water was so blue that it appeared black. She could just see her skin below the surface, bare and almost glowingly pale. She wondered why she wasn't wearing a swimsuit. The water was cold. Goosebumps covered any part of her skin that rose above the water, even momentarily. She leaned back, so just her face was above the surface. Then she felt it, the water around her was moving. There was something swimming up from below her, rising closer in circles that grew ever smaller around her. It was something big, and it was coming for her, for her specifically. She looked up at the sky, and it was filled with stars, they sparkled like ice, like broken glass on pavement.

It was coming closer. The temperature of the water dropped even more. It was right below her. She woke up, her body jolting like it sometimes did when she dreamed of falling.

Karynn looked around her, feeling dizzy, and for a second couldn't place where she was. Nothing was familiar. She turned on the bedside lamp and remembered that she was in the apartment.

Karynn got out of bed and went to the bathroom to splash her face. She turned on the tap and heard something. It was a woman crying. Or that's what it sounded like.

There was a distinct sob. It was coming from the hallway. She walked to the apartment door and peeked out the peephole. The lights in the hallway were off. She didn't know they turned off at night, must have been some conservation thing.

The sob again. This time it seemed choked, gurgly. She thought about going into the hallway. She really should check, she thought, to make sure someone wasn't hurt, wasn't looking for help. She undid the deadbolt and the security latch. She reached for the doorknob and thought she heard waves. She jumped, startled. The sobbing had stopped as well. It must not have been anything; she must have imagined it after the dream. She redid the deadbolt and security latch. She went back to bed.

At work the next day, Karynn was able to forget about the night before. She carried the memory of the dream, but more like a thin coat, something that could be forgotten while it was being worn. There was a case involving a contractual dispute. It wouldn't end up in court if she played her cards right. She had chosen contracts as her specialty because she thought it might be a path where she could solve the majority of her cases without going to court.

The key to contracts was understanding the flaws not necessarily in logic but in the opposite of logic, she thought. Finding ways around a contract needed a certain type of mind, a madness method. There was always a loophole. There was always a way out if one knew the right way to look.

There was a breeze in her office, it ruffled papers on her desk. The ruffling of paper against of paper. It sounded like water a little. It sounded like waves.

Karynn opened her eyes. She was on a tiny raft in the middle of water. The water was endless. It had no end, just met the sky on and on forever, in every direction. She stared up at the sky, and the sun was beaming down. Everything was so bright. The reflections off the water glinted like flashlights in mirrors. She let one hand dip into the water. The water was warm from the sun. It seemed so peaceful. Except there was something coming towards her. It was beneath the water, but she could see ripples on the water, tiny waves. It was circling her. The circles were so close. She lifted her hand out of the water. She curled into a ball in the middle of the raft. Maybe, it wouldn't know she was there. She tried to not even breathe. The raft beneath began to rock. It was there.

Karynn opened her eyes, spinning slightly in her chair. She had never had the dream during daylight before.

When she returned to the apartment building, she paused in the hallway outside the apartment. She looked up at the lights. They beamed brightly. She wondered if they had really been off the night before or if the whole thing had been an extension of her dream. She wondered if she should see a specialist. Was it normal to have a nightmare recur for years?

As she was staring at the door, Davis came out of his apartment. "Hey, Karynn."

She turned to face him. "Oh, hey, I was just going inside."

"Yeah, look, you didn't, like, see Lucy last night or today at all?" he asked.

"Lucy? Not after the party thing. No," she said.

"We had a little argument, and she said she was going to get something last night. And she didn't come back. She's probably crashing at some friends. Teach me a lesson or whatever."

Karynn thought that this sounded plausible. Lucy had seemed like the sort of woman who probably would go in for a dramatic lesson. There had been the sobbing woman, though, but that had been a dream. "Did you try calling her?"

"Yeah, she, she doesn't pick up, though. Even when she's happy with me. So..." Davis shrugged.

"Well, if I see her, I'll let you know," Karynn wanted to go inside. She began to unlock her door.

"Yeah, please do, thanks. I'm going to ask around the building, too, just in case."

Karynn nodded and slipped inside the apartment. She thought of the sobbing, the choked gurgle. She tried to shake the thought away.

As she was making supper, someone knocked on the door. She almost didn't hear it over the music she had playing, trying to overrun the sounds in her head. She went to get the door. It was Laurence. He was looking artfully disheveled, again, she hated her mind for the description. He had on jeans and a shirt, slightly untucked, with his hair tousled.

"Hey, Karynn," he said. She tried to pick his accent out more. Maybe it wasn't British. Irish?

"Hey, did you need something?" she asked. She felt oddly nervous and crossed her arms across her chest, though she knew this belied her nervousness more than made her look strong.

"I was walking past, and I heard your music. I just wanted to warn you. The board of tenants, they're really, really finicky about music levels. And one of the most finicky lives next to you. Miss Grever. She won't be home for a bit, but I'd turn it down a little." He leaned against her doorframe.

"Oh, okay, thanks. I didn't realize it could be heard. I should really read those rules, I guess."

Laurence's eyebrows jumped on his face—a look of shock that might have registered as almost comical if it hadn't come with a slight paling of his skin. "You haven't read the rules?"

"No, since I was just apartment-sitting. It's not permanent, and there seemed to be so many. It's a whole handbook."

"I'd go ahead and read it, Karynn. I'd read it soon." Laurence no longer leaned. He was standing, and she realized he was at least a foot taller than her. It was intimidating, though it hadn't been the night before.

"I'll do that, then. I'm going to go read it right now," she said.

"Do. The rules, you know, they're important," he said.

Karynn nodded and began to close the door, then she asked before she could stop herself, "Hey, you haven't seen Lucy, have you?"

Laurence's look changed again. It became slightly darker. "No, no, I haven't. Not since last night."

"At the party?" Karynn wished her mouth would stop asking questions.

"Yes, at the party," Laurence said. "I've got to go, Karynn. But I'll see you later."

"Yeah," she said. She shut the door, making sure to click the deadbolt into place and reattach the security latch.

She went back to the kitchen and switched off her music. Silence fell around her. She went to get the rule handbook from the desk where Micah had left it. She remembered him mentioning it in a joking manner. *Remember to read all the rules. You have to read all the rules.* She had thought it was a joking manner.

She opened it. There were 333 rules. They ranged from noise policies to what someone could hang on their door. She paged through to the last page, rule number 333. It was a simple one: *Do not leave your apartment between 1AM and 4AM. The lights will not be on for you.*

Karynn set the book down, planning to find another place to live in the morning.

She was underwater. She opened her eyes, and water was all around. Her hair billowed around her head. It obscured her view, but she knew something was there with her. It was swimming right next to her. She broke the surface of the water, gasping in mouthfuls of air. She screamed for help. She was in the middle of the sea. There was no one. Something touched her feet. It was right next to her.

She screamed, sitting up in bed. Someone was pounding on her door, yelling for help. She stepped out of bed, walking into the front room and switching on the light. She ran to the front door. She looked at the clock placed directly above the door. It was 2AM. She hesitated.

"Please, please, someone," Davis' voice said. He sounded terrified—more than terrified, crazed by terror. He banged on the door again. Then she heard a sound like something running on all fours across the hallway. Pets weren't allowed—rule number 3. "No, no, no!"

She heard whimpering. Then a dragging. She stared at the door. What was wrong with her? She undid the lock and opened the door. She stepped out into the darkened hallway. Light from her apartment, though, spilled out, and so she could see. Davis was curled in a ball on the floor, whimpering, covered in his own blood. A shape crouched over him. It was a woman in a long dress. She was beautiful. Marissa. She crouched on all fours, and it took Karynn a moment to realize what was so strange. Marissa's hands and feet looked natural, with all four on the floor.

"You shouldn't have come out. We have rules," Marissa said, in that not beautiful voice.

"What's going on?" Karynn asked. The question sounded so weak. She wanted to run back inside, but couldn't move.

"Davis broke the rules. He and his little Lucy have been making a lot of noise. Noise carries. It's impolite to your neighbors," Marissa said. She had still not raised her head, staring intently at Davis.

"So, you attacked him?" Karynn asked. Why hadn't she called the police?

"He broke the rules, Karynn. You can't just do that. We have a board of tenants. We keep this a nice place." Marissa slipped one of her hands around Davis' neck, beginning to squeeze as he whimpered. Blood oozed out where Marissa's fingernails were digging into his skin. Karynn did the only thing she could think of. She ran up to Marissa and punched her as hard as she could. She had never punched anyone. She wasn't sure that she had ever even thought of punching anyone.

Marissa pushed Davis's head to the side in a quick jerk movement, a tiny snap that Karynn barely heard, and stood straight up in a smooth movement. She slapped Karynn, and the blow felt like being hit with a mallet. Karynn fell backwards. She felt blood coming from her nose. It dripped hot down her face.

"You don't hit the chair of the board of tenants, Karynn. You're breaking a lot of rules." Marissa said, and she raised her head as she did. Karynn saw her face. It was the same perfectly proportioned, beautiful face. Marissa smiled and opened her mouth, gone were the even and white teeth. Her mouth opened far wider than a human mouth should ever open, revealing rows of shark-like teeth, jagged and long. They were still sparklingly white. "We created a nice place here, Karynn. We want to keep it that way. Don't you like it here? Isn't this a nice place for working singles?"

Karynn tried to move. The pain in her head was intense. "What are you going to do to me?"

"Well, you broke the rules. And that means I get to devour you."

Karynn blinked, pain blinding her. She couldn't have heard that right. "Devour me?"

Marissa stepped closer. "Yes, devour you. Break the rules, and I get to do what I think is a rightful punishment. It's in the contract, Karynn."

Karynn sat up. The blood rushed down from her nose, coating her chin. She could taste it. "What contract?"

"Every tenant signs it when they get the handbook of rules." Marissa smiled. Her teeth glistened.

Karynn wanted to laugh. It bubbled up inside her, with something close to the hysterical. "I'm not a tenant."

Marissa stood directly over her. She dropped to all fours, tilting her head to look Karynn in the face. "What?"

"I didn't sign the contract. I'm apartment-sitting. By extension, if I break rules, I'm not in breach of contract; the person who let me apartment-sit is."

Marissa's eyes widened. They were so deep and so dark, like the sea. "You didn't sign the contract." She paused, pondering. "So, you're saying that Micah is the one in breach of contract?"

Karynn thought about it for a second. He was a friend of a friend. She didn't know him that well, at all. "Yeah, that's what I'm saying. Rules are important. You should stick to your contracts."

"Rules are important." Marissa lowered her head for a moment. She was thinking. "You didn't break the contract. When is Micah coming back?"

"Two weeks," Karynn whispered.

"I can wait two weeks. Rules need to be kept," Marissa said. She turned and walked, all four feet padding against the ground, back to Davis' body. She gripped his arm with her teeth and began to drag the body away. Karynn fell back against the floor. She lay there for a while before crawling back to the apartment. Micah's apartment.

She packed up the next morning and moved out. She'd stay on the floor of a cousin's flat for a while. It wasn't a particularly nice building, but she was fine with that.

She didn't talk to Micah again. She never called or sent a note. She didn't want to know for sure that there wouldn't be an answer.

She sometimes argued cases in court. She was surprisingly fierce, the other lawyers would remark. She still preferred to settle out of court, though.

Once in a while, the dream returned to her. She'd be floating on the surface of the water, and something would keep getting closer to her. Sometimes she would look down into the darkness of the water. Sometimes she would see what was swimming up towards her, through the black water. The thing looking up at her from the darkness was always her own face. She kept getting closer and closer.

Woman in the Garden

There once was a girl. They called her Vervain, though she never knew if this was what her parents had intended her to be named or if it was merely the name that was placed upon her once she had been given to the Gardeners. The Greenhouses were large, and as a child, she was allowed to roam freely among them. She could not remember a time before knowing the heat of the greenhouses. It was a specific heat that pressed down into her and made her lungs feel heavy within her chest. Sometimes, she would step outside just to take in gulps of air that wasn't humid. She liked the way it chilled her throat, raised goosebumps along her arms. As she grew older, she grew more accustomed to the heat, and trips to the outside became less and less frequent.

Vervain found that she dreamed of plants. She would be walking amongst the Greenhouse rows, and the plants would speak to her or invite her to dance or, occasionally, they would reach out and wrap their leaves around her in an embrace. She would wake up and run to the plant-beds. She would press her ear to the earth, but she could never hear what the plants might have been whispering.

When she was twenty-five, the head Gardeners came to her and told her that she would be given a Greenhouse of her own. There came rules with the guardianship of a Greenhouse. She could not break the rules. There could be no new plants introduced, there could be no unofficial visitors, and the produce had to be given only to those who were on the list. Vervain agreed to the rules without question. Her heart beat faster at the thought of being able to spend even more time caring for the plants.

She woke every morning slightly before the sun cast its rays through the Greenhouse glass. She liked the calm of the darkened Greenhouse. The plants were still asleep, and she would tiptoe amongst them. She sometimes would press her fingers into the soil of the beds. She liked the pressure it took to slide her finger in: fingertip and then up to her first joint, then the next, then to her knuckles. She could tell easily when the plants would need watering next. She had to be sparing with the water. The filtering process to avoid cross-contamination was costly and took a long time. Or so she was told repeatedly. She checked the plants for dead leaves and would pluck them off. Her movements became faster, her pinching ability more refined. She didn't want the plants to feel her nails cutting quick into their skin.

The first inspection came, and the Officials took samples of her plants. They had tiny scissors, vials, and little strips of measuring tape. Vervain could not watch as they snipped, measured, and removed pieces. She felt her hands trembling and curled her fingers inward to her palms, forming fists until her own fingernails pierced them.

The Officials asked her questions: Have you allowed anyone inside? Do you bring in outside plants? Who watches the Greenhouse when you are not here? No, and no, and I am never not here, she responded. Do you give away any of the plants? She startled at that one, the thought of handing them away like handing away her own children would feel.

Everyone knew what the food outside the Greenhouses did to you. It wasn't like this was a new thing. It wasn't like unpredictability had been thrown in. Predictability was the key to the food outside the Greenhouses. It had been created to be predictable. So, of course, what it did to a person's body must also then be predictable. Or predictable eventually, as everyone was told. Predictable eventually. Vervain had heard the stories; she had seen the children who had never tasted a Greenhouse tomato or could even imagine the perfection of imperfection that a tomato could have. She knew that they probably never would taste one either. The Government regulated the Greenhouse food; the recommendations were that it was too late for most people, and so only the untainted could be allowed to eat of the Greenhouse bounty. Only unpredictable results could come from feeding the tainted with the Greenhouse food. Unpredictable and costly results. There simply wasn't enough of the Greenhouse produce for everyone, was there?

Vervain had grown up with the rules and the speeches. She had memorized them and could have repeated them verbatim even in her dreams if she was ever called upon to do so. She knew what crops grew outside the safety and the glass and the security of her Greenhouse. Those stalks out there, so tall and symmetrical, and those plants hung low with the bulging red tomatoes, perfect spheres of red like the sun would look if the sun burned crimson. She knew when she went outside. She had to scrub her skin, her clothing before she could return to the greenhouses. The outside pollens clung to the flesh, to fabric, as if they had small claws hidden in their particles. She sometimes scrubbed until her own skin flushed red. Cross-contamination was what everyone feared. It had been the purpose once, of course. The trick, the trap, the clanging shut of a locked gate.

Her days become increasingly rhythmical. She woke, she tended, she watered, she slept. Repeat. Repeat. Repeat. One morning, she woke up, and the plants were speaking. She knew she was dreaming, and so she eavesdropped in on them. They spoke of the sun and how they had never felt it, but that they remembered it. That the memory of its beauty and its grace and its heat had germinated inside them. They spoke of how they had never felt rain or the wind. They longed for the songs of cicadas and the feel of tiny tree frog toes, sticky and soft, climbing up their limbs and nestling among their leaves. The plants sang of these songs and whispered of them, and then they wept. They wept and wept, and Vervain felt them weeping deep within her.

She woke and tended the plants, but their leaves shrank from her touch. She pressed her ear to the dirt amongst them, and it smelled of salt, of tears dried.

She slept and again she dreamt of them singing and whispering and weeping of all the earth that they would never know.

She woke and went to her favorite plant. The amaranth, Love-Lies-Bleeding, and she carefully dug her fingers into the soil around it. She dug and dug until she had dug a space next to it. She climbed up onto the plant beds. She lay down in the spot she had dug. She nestled into the earth, both cool and yet warm. She closed her eyes and thought of the Outside. She thought of the sun and of rain and of wind and of how it must have once been. She tried to dream it beautiful for the plants. She tried to make it seem as beautiful as it was in stories, as it used to be back and back and backwards in time. She breathed in. The earth around her smelled sweet and thick and alive. She slept, and the plants dreamt with her.

Symbiosis

After it happened, after we'd all slipped into its grip, I would try to remember the last true moment I'd had. I'd been looking out the bay windows. A ship was coming closer, getting ready to dock. They'd flagged us a few hours previously so they could deliver something. One of the station scientists had been awaiting whatever it was for months. The excitement in the research team was palpable. It felt like the air was filled with something: it felt like static and tasted like copper, like the air before lightning.

"What do you think it is?" Kieran asked me. I hadn't noticed him approaching, and so I jumped slightly, my shoulders rising defensively before I could stop myself.

"I don't know," I said. I kept my voice even, trying not to play up the moment of fear.

I turned from the window to face him. He was looking out the window, not at me. It was rare to get a moment where he wasn't matching my gaze, and so I let myself glance at the scar that stretched from his hairline, down his cheek, charting the length of his neck, before finally dipping under his shirt. The scar was almost shockingly white against his skin. It looked like a star falling through the night sky. He never talked about the accident that left him alive but marked. But others talked about it, in whispers mostly, because he was the sole survivor of a crash. The whole crew dead and him, a miracle in the wreckage. We had words for what he was, but they all came down to this: we considered him a luck charm. Catastrophes in space were small— more on pods or if you were a jumper, but rarely on ships or stations—and so having someone who'd been through one already, on board, it pretty much meant that it wouldn't happen again. Not while they were on board. I wondered how he felt about that, to be such an unlucky symbol of luck. Where did the scar stop? I traced it in my mind, under his shirt, across his skin.

He turned back to me, but I'd already averted my gaze to down the hallway. "It's about to dock," he said.

"Kit, report to the research bay," Alexa told me through the intercom. It was early in the morning. Like crack of dawn back home early. Still, I dragged myself up and out to the research bay, without even the dark mutterings that normally would have hovered in my mouth. I had the kind of curiosity about what had been delivered that fairy tales used to warn against.

The research bay was buzzing. Not metaphorically. Literally, a buzzing sound filled the air just below the level of everyone's voices. The four scientists, currently in the station's rotation, were standing around some kind of aquarium. Dr. Ambrose turned to me as I entered. She was the one I knew best, as we'd talked over meals a few times. Her research had to do with water, something about fluidity and dynamics.

"Kit, excellent." She beckoned me over. "Drs. Lewis, Jones, and Escalante, this is Kit D'Etcheverry. She's the best of the techs on board."

I smiled, tried to force myself to blush so that I'd seem humble. But it was true. I knew every operating system in the fleet, could take them apart and put them back together blindfolded. I could crack codes in seconds. "Thank you, Dr. Ambrose."

Dr. Lewis stepped forward to shake my hand, and then I saw what the aquarium held. I felt myself involuntarily intake a gasp of air. Inside the water were four objects that looked like tubes mixed with mushroom stalks. Some kind of sea life, except they glowed. The amount of light was more than some kind of bioluminescence that didn't need the darkness to work. It was as if they were holding sunlight itself. The doctors laughed at my reaction, but I was too busy stepping forward, not blinking, watching the light. "What is it?"

"Have you ever heard of a Venus Flower Basket?" One of the doctors asked.

I shook my head.

"Well, that's too bad, because this is sort of like that. It's a kind of bioluminescent sponge. These aren't those exactly, but the shape, color, and growth are similar."

"Where is it from?" But I knew. Everything in me, as I leaned forward to study it, knew.

"The goldilocks. It was one of the samples collected. We're the team getting to do some preliminary study on it, before they decide if they'll transport some back to Earth," a doctor said.

The sponge pulsed out light. It felt warm on my skin. I wanted to reach out and touch the glass, to feel the heat, let it pool into me. I turned from it, back to the doctors. "And what do you need from me?"

"We need someone to help us set up a program to study it. We essentially want something that can help us monitor the light and pulses, even when we're not in the room. And then, also, help figure out if there is a pattern, etc." Ambrose said. She looked back at the sponge and a smile curled at the corners of her lips. I wondered if she, too, wanted to reach out and touch the glass, feel the warmth seep into her skin. It would have felt so good.

I nodded. It would be a simple thing to set up. I could do it in my sleep.

That night, I dreamt of biking down a suburban street at night. Every house was dark, and there were no streetlights. I didn't know where I was going, but as I biked, the wind rushing against me, the houses began to glow from within. They slowly got brighter and brighter. Brighter. The light caressed my skin, slipped inside me. My body thrummed with it, and I woke up gasping.

"So you're the lucky one, huh?" I was eating breakfast when Kieran approached me. He sat down across from me after asking.

"Lucky one?"

"You're working with the delivery. What is it?" He leaned forward, eager to hear. He had perfectly shaped eyes. Something

I'd never noticed before. They were spaced a little further apart than most people, giving him an open look.

"It's some kind of water plant," I said.

"A water plant?"

I lowered my voice, leaned closer to him, "from the goldilocks."

His eyes widened. "I knew it had to be. They were being so secretive. But I also didn't quite believe it. What is it like?"

"It's kind of…I don't know. It's some kind of sponge. One of the scientists said it reminded them of A Venus Flower Basket." I said.

"Oh, till death do us part," he said.

"What?" I didn't even try to hide the confusion in my voice.

He smiled. "It's what they supposedly symbolize. I had a friend who specialized in sponges, if you can believe that that's something people specialize in."

"I could show it to you tonight, if you want? I have to take some notes on its light emission."

"Okay, I'd like to do that with you," he replied. For a split moment, I wanted to reach out and touch him, but I didn't know why.

In the research bay, I was the only one there. The aquarium still glowed, and I turned off the overhead lights for a moment to watch it. The color shimmered, accepting the darkness in, and then intensified to make up for it. I placed a hand against the glass. It was warm like the outside of a cup of tea, hot enough to yell caution but not hot enough to make me take my hand away.

"Jesus."

I spun around at Kieran's voice in the dark, my heart beating too fast. He was right behind me. I could feel the warmth of his body. "I didn't hear you come in."

"I didn't mean to scare you," he said. "I just saw you standing there and the light…"

"The light?"

He shrugged, "It just made you look different, I guess. I wanted to see you up close." He turned to the aquarium. I reached out and took his hand, placing it against the aquarium glass. He gasped, under his breath.

I wanted to ask him thought, but instead we stood there, letting the light caress us as the heat pulsed through our skin.

We stood there for I don't know how long before he finally pulled away. "I should let you work."

I nodded, switching on the overhead light. It was so dim compared to what we had just seen. The stalks of the plant lowered their own radiance in response. We blinked a few times, accustoming our eyes.

"Thank you for showing me," Kieran said. He slid his hand from the aquarium, brushing my fingers with his own as he did. Then he left me alone with the light.

In the morning, I saw Dr. Ambrose in the lab, and so I stepped in to talk to her. "Hey, I just wanted to say thank you for bringing me into the program."

She didn't look up from what she was studying at her desk. "Ambrose?" I said, a little louder. Her body jolted, startled, and she looked up. A blush bloomed across her cheeks.

"Oh, Kit, sorry, I was just…Well, daydreaming about my husband." She shook away whatever the thought had been.

"It must be hard, being away for so long," I said.

She nodded. "Yes, I keep dreaming about him. I never used to." She paused, maybe embarrassed to continue. "So what do you need, Kit?"

"I just wanted to say thanks for bringing me in on the program."

She smiled, her gaze already slipping away from mine, back to some memory. I'd never seen her so unfocused. "Yes, of course. Great job."

I nodded, didn't remind her that I'd barely started. "Okay, thanks, again." I left, walking through the research station. A couple of the scientists were standing close to the aquarium, their bodies pressed together as they leaned in, whispering something I couldn't hear. I watched them for a moment and then looked away. It felt, for some reason, like I was spying on something intimate, so I left.

…

That night, I went back for more data. I kept the light on, trying not to distract myself from the task at hand. After a few hours, though, I could barely keep my eyes open. My body felt tense. I heard the doors whoosh open and I looked up.

Kieran was there, carrying a coffee. "I walked past and saw you, thought you could use this."

"I can. So much." I took the cup and, again, our hands met. It was like someone was running fingertips over my whole body, instead of just a brush of our skin. "Thank you."

I took a sip, and we both turned to look at the aquarium. The light was different again. The stalks seemed to be pulsing it out faster.

"God, it's beautiful," Kieran said. "We should see it in the dark again."

I turned off the overhead, and the stalks pulsed faster and brighter. I could feel the heat of the glass, even from a few steps back. We both stepped forward at the exact same moment. And then we were touching the glass at the same time.

Our fingers touched, and I felt a jolt of static shock slip up through me. The glass felt hot, the warmth went into my skin, up my arm, and then all over me. I watched Kieran, watched the heat pool into him as well. He reached out and touched my face. Another surge of electricity. And then we were both touching the other. Our lips were touching, skin touching. His hands were around my waist. I pushed my hands up under his shirt, his skin was so hot, like a fever coursed through him. And then we were on the floor, our clothes off, and I was tracing the arc of his scar with my lips. The air throbbed with electricity, with sparks. It felt exactly like a lightning storm now, the buzzing taste of the air. His hands on me felt far away, and so I pulled him closer as he pushed into me. I saw the lights spooling out from the glass like tendrils, saw them making patterns in the air above us. It looked like the lights were dancing.

...

Back in my bed, I tried to think over what had happened. There were so many protocols I'd just broken. It made me dizzy to think about. I tried not to focus on Kieran, on how he had felt, on the taste of him as I'd kissed his skin.

I slipped into a dream where I was on a ship out on the sea. There was a storm, and I was tossed over into the water. Sinking, women swam around me with shimmering fish tails, they grabbed hold of my arms, and I thought they were going to save me. But they just pulled me deeper.

...

In the morning, I woke up groggy. My limbs were heavy, as if I'd taken a sleeping pill before going to bed. In the corridor, I walked past two crew members. They were standing close together, and it was only as I passed them that I saw it was because they were kissing.

As I passed the research bay, I looked in and saw Dr. Ambrose leaning against the aquarium. Her face pressed against the glass, it looked like she had been crying, but in a happy way, as if she'd just seen someone she'd loved and lost and now had returned miraculously to her.

Across the research station, another pair of scientists was holding each other. Their embrace so tight that it seemed as if they were being tied together by something. I wanted to look, but everything in me was heavy, sluggish.

I kept walking until I reached Kieran's room. I knocked once, and he opened. "I was just, I was just coming to find you," he said.

"Something's wrong," I said. "It's doing something."

He reached out and pulled me to him. His body was warm, safe. I just wanted to be held by him forever. "It's fine. It's fine."

We walked to his bed and he pulled me onto it with him.

I thought of the women pulling me deeper under the waves and I tried to fight the feeling. But like drowning, I knew at some point to give in.

"What's happening?" I asked as he hugged me closer. I put my arms around him, gave in to the embrace. It felt so comfortable, so right.

But he didn't answer. He was already gone.

It was luck, really, that they found us at all. A passing ship noticing that we didn't answer any signals. I heard about it later. How everyone on board was asleep, wrapped in each other's embraces. "You all looked so peaceful, I almost felt bad saving you," someone said to me.

They quarantined us. Quarantined the plant or whatever it was. I dream of it sometimes still, the light was the most beautiful thing I ever witnessed or would witness.

We don't know exactly what it was doing to us, though the doctors said we were low on certain nutrients in our system. So maybe it was just hungry.

I heard later that Ambrose was the only one not found with someone else. I found out she was a widow sometime after. That her husband had died shortly before she joined our ship. She had looked so happy daydreaming about him, and I hope I can never understand what that would be like—dreaming about the one you loved after they were erased from you.

Kieran and I married a couple of years ago. It was a small ceremony, and everyone commented on how, in the vids of it, we looked so happy, so in love. When I look into his eyes, I see the world I want to be in.

But, sometimes, I can't help but think back to before the lights. To that moment when I think it couldn't yet have affected us, and I was looking at him, marveling at the scar against his skin. I must have wanted him then, I'm sure.

I'm sure, and yet everyone who woke up in the arms of someone that day, when they were saved, must have thought the same thing—all that light in their lovers' eyes.

A Knocking Almost Like Hands

Once upon a time, in a little house, the children were sleeping. In the little house, everything was quiet, there was no one awake but someone was moving.

There was someone in her house. Miranda could feel her heart pounding in her chest, and she tried to block the sound out so that she could listen for footsteps. Silence. Getting out of bed as stealthily as she could, she creeped to the bedroom door. Silence. Pressing her ear against the door, heart thump-thumping in her head, she tried to block out everything but what she had thought she heard. Now, she wasn't sure what it was that woke her: a floorboard creaking downstairs, an object clattering to the ground, or maybe someone muttering something under their breath. She only knew that there was *something* that had woken her. Still, there was only silence from the rest of the house. After a few moments of nothing, she finally went back to sleep.

In the morning, she had forgotten completely about it. Or if she did remember it, it was as a sort of dream mixed with a memory of her childhood home—someone yelling and a sound like creeping, creeping.

"Miranda?" Carolyn asked, voice hitting the higher pitch that signaled she was annoyed.

"Yeah?"

Carolyn sighed. "Where is your head today? I've asked you about the Carter report six, maybe seven, times now."

Miranda knew that Carolyn's six times was another person's twice. "Sorry, Carolyn. Just been tired lately. Maybe not sleeping well?"

Carolyn nodded, trying to work a sympathetic look onto her face. "Oh, you poor thing. It's so hard being in an empty house. Any word on when Liv will be back?"

Everyone asked her that, constantly, as if she could predict the way that wars worked. Liv was a photojournalist and she went where she was told for as long as she was told. "You know, I'm not sure."

"Maybe you should invite someone to stay with you? Until she gets back? Isn't your brother…" Carolyn peered intently at Miranda, waiting for her to fill in the statement: isn't your brother…a bit of a mess? Always needing a place to stay? Hard up? Carolyn leaned closer, waiting for Miranda to fill in the blanks in a way that would give her a gossipy-kick. Miranda often did want to give Carolyn a kick, but not the gossipy kind.

"I like being alone. It's quiet." Miranda turned to her desk, sorting through her pile of files until she'd found the Carter report. She didn't like talking about her brother as something for other people's entertainment. His problems were vast, but she found nothing to be gained in telling people them. He was her brother, as close to her own true self as anyone could be. "Here's that report."

Carolyn snatched it up. "Perfecto! The client's being a bit of wink wink nudge nudge, you know what I mean?"

It was highly likely that no one person could ever know what Carolyn meant. "Yeah, yeah, totally."

Carolyn smiled and walked away. The truth was, Miranda wasn't sure how she liked being alone. She hadn't been alone in a house by herself for years. Even in college, she'd always lived with a roommate until she met Liv. She'd been looking forward to the space and quiet so much. But there was just so much of it.

Miranda returned her gaze to her computer screen, waking it by moving the mouse. The screen turned back on and on it was an open Word document. Eight words were typed, the beginning of a sentence that Miranda had no memory of typing: *Once upon a time, in a little house.* The words reminded her, for some reason, of a fairy tale her mother used to tell her and her brother. In it, two bad little girls were always causing trouble for their mother and so she went away and the little girls came home to find a replacement mother. One with glass eyes that sparkled in the dark and long, long hands. Miranda had hated the story as a child, finding it terrifying. She couldn't not think about those long, long hands reaching out to grab her, bring her close to them. Her mother would always end the story by reminding Miranda and her brother to be good when their father came home or else the story might come true.

She frowned, deleting the words.

On the drive home from work, she stopped to get a coffee—fully knowing that she'd be working at home for longer than she wanted to. Her phone buzzed as she waited in line. A reminder that her father's birthday was coming up. *Get a good gift* her phone glared up at her. There was nothing she could get that her father would appreciate, every year she knew it and every year she tried to escape it. She'd remind herself earlier and earlier, spending hours poring over sites online—trying to find something, anything, that he'd not scowl at. He never flat-out said something rude, which she convinced herself she would have been able to take, he'd instead send her a note. *Thanks Miranda. This reminds me of you.* he had sent after she gave him an art print, a woodblock of a woman drowning. Or *It's nice to have a daughter with such a male fashion sense.* he'd written for a tie she'd sent him. And always, always, she could hear him in her head. His non-acknowledgment of Liv, the tiny barbs he had spread throughout Miranda's life. She had thought about ignoring him, cutting him out of her life, but somewhere she'd hear her mother telling them: you have to be good for your father or you're really just being cruel to me. And Miranda had known it was true.

At home, Miranda worked until it was almost nine. A pang in her stomach reminded her that she'd never eaten dinner. In the kitchen, the faucet was on. A steady stream of water splashing into the sink. Miranda quickly turned it off. It had to have been on for hours, since she got home. Though she couldn't remember having turned it on or why she would have.

While she was fixing a sandwich, the phone rang. "Hello?"

"Mandy?" A man's voice asked.

"Uh, no…" Miranda said. She hadn't gone by Mandy since she was a child. She'd hated it as a nickname, it never made sense as an abbreviation of Miranda. Her father insisted on calling her this, saying she hadn't earned the name Miranda yet.

"Sorry, I swear this was her number," the man said.

"No problem," Miranda hung up the phone. It was an odd coincidence.

Behind her, someone laughed. Miranda spun around, still clutching the knife from her sandwich-making. No one was there. She didn't think of herself as a susceptible person, but here she was, alone in her own home, jumping at imagined noises.

She returned to her study, closing the door behind herself. A habit she stayed in even when Liv wasn't there. She needed some spots that were completely hers, shut away and alone.

For a few moments, she listened for wrong sounds— anything that might mean someone else was in the house with her. There was nothing and somehow the silence was even more unnerving. She turned on her stereo, blasting music to chase away the nothing.

She worked on reports for hours more. She worked until the exhaustion swarmed up around her, digging into her skin with its nails. She closed her eyes and saw rows of figures. Her ears buzzed. She stumbled to bed, happy to be tired enough to not dream.

Once upon a time, in a little house, the children were sleeping. In the little house, everything was quiet, there was no one awake but someone was moving. It was not quite anyone, what with those long fingers and those empty eyes. Oh they emptied out all the way into shadows.

"I'm not," someone said.

Miranda sat up in bed. For a moment, she swore someone was sitting on the very edge of the bed. A dark shape staring down at the floor. She blinked rapidly, clearing away the possibility of a dream imprint. No one was there.

"Hello?" Miranda said, quiet, feeling silly for doing so.

Silence.

She settled back into her pillows, listening hard in case she could hear something else. There was nothing. No one. She turned on her side and watched as an indentation in the pillow next to hers slowly exhaled back into its normal state.

In the morning, Miranda walked around the house before work. She checked that everything was still locked from the inside. No one could have been in the house with her and yet, she still couldn't shake the feeling that someone definitely had been.

It was Saturday and so she had the day to herself. She went to her study and began to review some case files. She kept, for some reason, thinking about the stories her brother and she used to tell. They always made up ghost stories to entertain one another. They'd pretended the house was haunted.

Her computer dinged. A video chat call. She'd forgotten that Liv was supposed to call. She accepted and the screen filled with a fluttering image of Liv. Even that, the imperfect image of Liv, made Miranda's heart leap into her throat. She ached.

"Hey, love," Liv smiled, her image glitching for a second, so her smile seemed held for an unnaturally long time. The connection was never very good.

"Hi," Miranda was never good at interacting on video calls. She always felt strangely exposed, even more so than when talking in person. Liv looked different. Her hair was tied up loosely and strands stuck up here and there, a streaking of gold shimmered along the top of her head from where she'd been in the sun too much. A dark bruise arced across her face. "Jesus, what's that from?"

Liv frowned. "What?"

"The bruise!" Miranda couldn't stand looking at it. It seemed to grow darker with each second. It seemed to pulse, as if wanting to consume the rest of Liv's face into its own darkness.

"This?" Liv reached up and touched the mark. "Just a little bruise. I'm surprised you can even see it. I was elbowed at the market the other day. Long story, but—" The image on the screen froze. Liv's face distorted with black squares. They floated across her eyes on the screen. Miranda thought, what empty eyes just like—Then she pushed that thought from her head.

"Liv, you still there? You froze up?"

"I…I…Can…Hear you." Liv's voice went in and out, crackling. "Who…the house…"

"What? You're breaking up."

"The house…behind you. Who's…in the…with you?" The call failed.

Miranda turned around, heart pounding, just to check, and faced the closed door. For minutes, she stared at the door. The no one that was there. She waited for Liv to call back, for someone to break her out of the silence. Nothing happened.

…

Her brother was coming over for dinner that night. Miranda told herself that she'd invited him because she missed him. She knew, though, there was more than that behind it.

The doorbell rang at six. She jumped when it sounded, her brother was never on time.

Steven stood on her porch, staring off into the darkening street, as she opened the door. He turned, smiling, to her. "Hey, sis."

"Steven, come in!" They hugged. He was thinner than usual even. "How have you been?"

"Good, you know, got a new job." He said, as they walked through to the dining room.

"Yeah? That's great! Where?" she asked. She went to the kitchen to get the pasta.

His voice flickered through to her. "…for Dad's company."

Miranda went back to the dining room. "You're going to work for Dad?"

Steven shrugged. "Have to take anything I can get. He offered and so I said yes."

Their father ran a company that oversaw some kind of drilling operation. He'd rarely been home when they were little because of the work he did. It turned him into a ghost, almost, haunting their actions and thoughts even when he wasn't there. Just the presence their mother could use to threaten them into behaving. Just the presence who occasionally showed up to sigh at them and berate their mother about her failings with them. He wanted children who made something of themselves, that's what he'd said once. *They should be excelling already. Look at her, she's hardly even excelling at being a girl.* "Well, that's nice of him, I guess."

They began to eat, chatting about what they'd both been doing. At a pause in the conversation, Miranda finally asked what she'd wanted to since opening the door. "Do you remember when we were little and we thought the house was haunted?"

Steven paused, fork halfway to his mouth. "Uh, sort of."

"There were like sounds right? Like someone walking and you heard them talking?"

Steven shook his head. "No, I think it was you."

Miranda felt her heart begin to pound. "Me?"

"You know, you were the one who heard someone talking. The, what did you call it, the Not-person?"

Miranda's fork slipped in her fingers. Her palms felt itchy, hot, sweaty. "The Not-person?"

Steven laughed, remembering. "Yeah, it was crazy. You said it was someone who wasn't someone. That they were in the house but usually only when we weren't there. It liked to be alone, you said."

She remembered. Mostly she remembered how frightened she used to make herself as a kid. The sound of her own heartbeat in her ears had made her think someone was walking towards her in the dark. She'd shake sometimes all through the night, curled under her covers, until it was light enough to see that no one was in the room with her. She knew better than to call out for her mother, who wouldn't hear her, or, worse, on the nights when her father was home and would hear her. *Why is the only girl-thing you do the most annoying? Getting scared of shadows, Mandy. Pathetic.*

"You okay, Miran?" Steven asked, peering at her, concerned.

She nodded. "Just…I remembered it different, I guess."

"Why'd you bring it up, anyways?"

"Oh, just had a dream about it. Couldn't quite remember if it really happened." She cleared away their plates, hoping that Steven didn't see her hands trembling.

Had it started before or after that fairy tale their mother told them? She couldn't quite remember. The long, long hands. The mother who was not the mother. It made sense, if she broke it down in a clinical manner that she fixated on things that were not like they should be. Her father's voice in her head. *Not-girl.*

Once upon a time, in a little house, the children were sleeping. In the little house, everything was quiet, there was no one awake but someone was moving. It was not quite anyone, what with those long fingers and those empty eyes. Oh they emptied out all the way into shadows. It was someone and not. Not and someone. That's the way it liked it. It was hard to tell stories about things that weren't there even when they were. And it was.

"Mandy," someone said. Right next to her. The breath was warm on her face. It smelled sweet, like hard root beer barrel candies sucked down to nothing.

Miranda gasped, sitting up. She reached for the bedside lamp and snapped it on. No one was in the room. Her shirt was drenched in sweat. Had she been having a nightmare?

She got up and went around the house, turning all of the lights on. Every room was empty.

In the morning, she tried to call Liv. The video call wouldn't connect. She tried over and over. There were things she wanted to say. She needed Liv to reassure her, to say she'd be home soon, to say Miranda would not be alone.

The day stretched out and out. The phone rang in the evening and Miranda picked it up. "Hello?"

"Hello," someone said. The voice was familiar and not, like hearing the adult version of a childhood friend's voice after not having seen them for years.

"Who are you?" she asked.

"I'm not," said the someone.

Miranda hung up the phone. She thought about leaving, about staying at a hotel, about calling her brother. But he had a job now, he probably had some place he was living and it was comfortable and filled up with his life and he wouldn't want to come stay with her. She was being foolish, after all. She should like being alone. It was a sign of character. Her father had told her *Scared of being by yourself now? Get used to it Mandy. I'm sure you'll end up alone.*

She went to her study and tried to work on case files. Somewhere, in the house, a faucet turned on. She could hear it. She locked the study door. Someone was walking around below her. They were trying to be quiet or maybe it was nothing. She pressed her ear against the door. Maybe it was silence. No one made any noise.

Miranda went to bed, turning off the light, and tried to shut her eyes. She'd go to work in the morning. She'd be surrounded by people and that, even Carolyn, was better than being all by herself.

Someone knocked on the bedroom door. Miranda tried not to scream. She'd imagined it. She stepped out of bed and went to the door. There were no sounds on the other side. She took a breath in and opened the door.

There was not someone outside.

Alley-Oop

The ball is a city when it leaves my hands. Every line and nub a street or a building, a person minding their business. Every bounce, dribble, shot that rattled the rim of the hoop before sliding past net, was a storm for someone. In street ball, the rules rush together. It's trash talk and pressing against the opponents, back to chest, trying to push towards something like a dance where each partner doesn't know a melody.

In school, though, the rules are contracts. Coach shakes his head, lets out a sigh, if he sees you disregard something he'd told you. When I tell Marcus that his granny could hustle more than him, Coach shakes his head at me. The ball is just a ball when it leaves my hands, I can't imagine the space of it as it arcs through the air.

At home, my cousin is still living with us. He's been out of rehab for weeks, but Mom says he can't find his footing. His mom was my mom's sister. I'd call her my aunt, but I never met her. Mom says her sister was all rattlesnakes and glitter. My cousin has never heard my Mom say this, but once, he and I were playing a video game, and he said that his favorite snake was a rattlesnake pilot.

"Snakes can fly?" I said. And it comes out sounding like a joke, and I wish I'd been making one.

My cousin laughed. "It's a kingsnake. They're harmless but they look a lot like a rattlesnake, sometimes even live with them. Imagine being that snake, just hanging out with all these big badasses, and them all thinking you are, too."

"I think that's me on the court," I said.

The first time I'd held a basketball, I was four, and my Dad had passed it gently to me. In my hands, it was heavy and I dropped it. As it rolled away, I saw people climb up from the lines. They were holding hands and scrambling to get out of the line of the roll. Or so I thought, but when I picked up the ball to stop their tumbles, I saw that they were dancing. One of the people tipped a hat to me as they settled back into their lines.

My Dad was delighted by how I stared at the ball, mouth agape. "You're gonna be a baller!"

On the court, the ball was always just a ball in everyone's hands, until it was in mine. And then it was a symphony playing from inside its hollow, dancers and people just minding their business too in the hub and bub of the city. I'd seen a man carrying flowers once, a little girl yanking her mother's hand to steer their walk towards a bakery, a little dog playing fetch with his people in the park. All I saw in the ball was life bustling forward.

My cousin used to make paintings, but I never saw them. He said he painted people and then painted landscapes over them. He said, "I know they're there and that's all I need."

Coach pulls me aside after practice one night and asks how I'm doing. "You're always so good in practice, man."

But in games, the ball passed between hands so quickly that I never had enough time with it. There was no moments to just watch the city life unfold. "I'll work on it, Coach. I promise!"

At home, I practice in the driveway with the regulation hoop Dad had put up when I was in middle school. I shoot fast, barely give myself time to dribble. Just bounce, hit into my palm, and shoot. Bounce, hit, shoot. Every shot sinks. But I don't feel the rhythm. It's just a ball and a point.

My cousin watches me from the grass. He sips a bottle of soda. He likes glass bottles, says they feel like home to him. And my Mom shakes her head, sighs, says, "Really, now."

"How am I looking?" I ask him.

"You haven't missed once, bud."

At night, sometimes, I'd hear him from the guest bedroom. Crying so quiet that he must have hid under the covers to muffle the sound. Sometimes in the mornings, when I got up with the sun, for my run, he'd be pacing the kitchen in his socked feet.

"Do you play?" I ask him.

He was five years older than me but my Mom looked at him like he was five years younger. When he was in the hospital, before rehab, she'd held her phone in her hand all day long. She jumped every time it buzzed. She said, "We should have brought him in after Marcia." And my Dad would shake his head, say, "Don't think in could haves. He'll come back to us, now."

"Not well. Not like you," he says. "You're going to be somebody big with those skills."

When Coach sighs at me, shakes his head, I see the future spooling away from me. No college scholarship, no brightness. If someone read my palms they'd see bruises and calluses from dribbles and slams, and maybe that would obscure all the paths I maybe could take.

"Want to play?" I ask.

My cousin shrugs. He has a long stride, and broad palms. When I pass the ball to him he catches it with ease. He looks down at the ball, studies it with a frown. A flinch, almost.

I wonder if he'll paint again, if he'll stay with us until he can, if he'll find a way to climb out of the lines he'd been set into. He dribbles twice and passes the ball to me.

When I catch it, the surface burns my hands. I look down at the ball and I'm holding the sun. Flaming and orange and brilliant in its burning. My cousin is watching me, and I've never noticed how his eyes are always looking at something else and never right ahead, not really.

And though it keeps burning my hands, I keep ahold of the ball, hold it until I can see a city waking up in its sunrise. And I pass the ball back, wonder if he can catch it.

Please Keep In Mind the Closest Exit May Be Behind You

A coffin was being sent up a conveyer belt into the belly of the plane. Lia saw it from out of the corner of her eye through the airport window. Simple wooden coffin, no embellishments, no shine to the wood. The type of pine box that a funeral parlor would never have out on their showroom floor. She didn't know that the dead were shipped commercially, but then again it wasn't exactly the sort of thing that she'd have looked up. A few other passengers stared as well.

Lia, when she was a kid, would have thought it was a bad omen. Older, she shrugged away the thought. Her father, a veteran of war, was superstitious. He often said that when you least expect it is when the dead will swallow you whole.

"We'll begin boarding shortly, the plane is ready for us." The ticket taker said with the false cheer of someone who wanted to pretend they weren't on the third delay of the flight's expected departure. Lia tried to flash them an encouraging smile, but she worried it came out a grimace. Checking her message app, there was nothing new from her sister.

Lina had asked her to fly out as soon as she could, said that she needed help. They hadn't been in the same country in half a decade. Lia staying in the US, where their parents had immigrated to, and Lina returning to the county of their birth for university and then for work. When they were young, they had always been inside of each other's footsteps. Lia and Lina. Irish twins, but everyone mistook them for identical ones. Their dark hair and shadow names, their big eyes and lanky forms. They'd drifted apart slowly, an iceberg cleaved in half. It was birthday emails and video calls at Christmas and not much else.

Lina hadn't been clear what she needed help for, had only hinted. She'd been seeing someone, said she wanted to come home, needed to leave. Lia had thought of saying that she couldn't—she had work, her wife needed her home for something, she was three months pregnant. But she didn't say the first because she could always take time and she didn't say the second because Veronica would have encouraged her to go and she didn't say the third because they weren't telling anyone yet. They wanted to be sure everything would be fine.

The ticket agent was starting boarding. Lia checked that she had placed everything back in her bag. She had packed light, always packed light no matter where she went. Her clothes tightly rolled parcels, which is how their father had taught them. A notebook and pen, the habitual products of her years when she was in the field. She wondered if Lina was packing, what she would bring between countries.

Lia got in line with her boarding group, ticket scanned with a comforting beep of acknowledgment. All those ways that technology said we were still breathing had always delighted her—the automatic doors opening, the checkmark filling in when she had proved she was not a robot. Stepping from the bridge onto the plane, she made her way toward the back. In the very last row, a woman sat reading a book. She would have been unremarkable had it not been for how the book was held so upright as to perfectly obscure her face, just the book, no skin, and her wave of dark hair around it. Lia had the uncomfortable thought, for just a moment, that the woman didn't have a face at all behind it. She pushed it away, laughed at her childishness.

When they were children, Lina and she had played a game in the summers. They were allowed to stay out longer, playing in the forest and field near their parent's house. When it reached dusk, right before their mother would call them home, they'd play the same game. They'd never named it, but Lia always thought of it as *Monster* in her head. In the game, they had to try to sneak home without being spotted by whatever they'd decided was stalking them through the trees, the long grass of the field. The goal was to get home the fastest but still be sneaky. Lia became adept at ducking behind objects, rolling out of sight,

74

whenever she heard something (a bird? The wind?) rustling anywhere near her. Lina took a less graceful approach, and would belly crawl towards home. They'd always arrive just as darkness had almost completely fallen, covered in dirt, grass stuck to hair and clothes, and their mother would roll her eyes and sigh.

Lia almost always made it to their yard first, the safety of stepping over the barrier just in front of her, but she'd wait for Lina. Wait until she could see her there, and then they'd cross over the threshold together.

Lia slid into her seat, pushed her knapsack underneath the seat in front of her. She pulled her headphones out and placed them around her neck. Slipped her notebook into the seat back pocket in front of her. She took a moment to take note of the people already seated around her. Diagonally in front of her, a young man and woman who must have been a couple and barely into their twenties. The young woman played at a bracelet on her wrist, twisting it one way and then the other. In front of Lia, two older women were deep in conversation, chuckling. Directly across the aisle from her, a man and his daughter. The little girl held a bright green stuffed creature—a lizard or alligator, perhaps. She wondered how often the girl had flown, if she worried every time the flight attendant said, "Put your own mask on first."

It was a seven-hour flight. Long enough to get uncomfortable, not long enough for Lia to sleep well. The last time she'd taken it, she was a child. Her parents had booked their tickets in separate rows so each girl got a window to press their face against, see the world shrink away from them. Lina had loved the clouds. Lia liked seeing the plats of land broken up like puzzle pieces below them. The world made sense from so far above.

The final boarders straggled on, and a woman took the seat next to Lia. She was tall, athletic looking, with blonde hair tied up in messy bun. She did the slight smile of commiseration as she accidentally elbowed Lia when she went for her seatbelt. "Such small seats!"

Lia nodded. "No worries." She closed her eyes waiting for the ascent, listening to the flight attendant cheerfully going through all the safety precautions for if something terrible happened.

Lina's message had been brief. *I need your help, Lia.* Lia had thought at first that it might be a scammer. So she'd said, *prove you're you.* Without a moment's pause, the conversation bubbles had popped up in the app. *We need to get home before dark.* So Lia had asked her what was wrong. Each sentence a single staccato beat of vague information. *I was seeing someone. I need to leave. Need to go home. Please come get me.* Lia had offered to send her money, buy her a ticket home. But Lina had said, *Lia, I'm scared. Please come help me to come home. I can't do this myself.* So she'd bought a ticket.

When Lia opened her eyes, they were already in the air. She looked out at the city getting smaller and smaller beneath them. The sun was setting and its red glow made the buildings look like upside-down fireworks. When they were young, a shared childhood friend had asked them at a sleepover what they'd like to be if they didn't have to be human and Lina had said *I'd like to be a memory.*

"It's getting dark so fast," Lia's rowmate said as she gazed out the window. It had already dipped to darkness. Lia looked for the moon, but it was nowhere to be seen.

"Must be extra cloudy."

"Must be. I'm Sara, by the way." The woman smiled at Lia. Lia had never been one to strike up conversations with other people on planes, even when she was a journalist, planes were her place where she could slip into her own mind.

"Lia," she said. Sara stared at her expectantly for a moment, as if expecting her to keep talking, to ask a question, to invite conversation in. But when Lia said nothing else, Sara returned to her tablet. She had a photo album open on it, and was scrolling through pictures of some sunny destination.

We need to get home before dark. Why had Lina used that phrase to prove that she was who she was? *Monster.*

A jolt of the plane and Lia felt her stomach drop like on a rollercoaster. A few people let out yips of surprise. The little girl across the aisle clutched her animal tighter.

"Sorry folks, just a little turbulence tonight," the pilot said over the intercom. "We should be finding our way out shortly. In the meantime, we're going to turn on the seatbelt sign and ask that you remain seated."

Outside the sky was now complete blackness. Lia looked for flickers of light from below, cities lighting up the dark, but there was nothing. The cabin lights had already been dimmed, just the light blue glow of the safety line above. From a few rows behind her, Lia heard someone humming. A low and rhythmic sound. Like the sound a child might make to soothe themselves, but all grown up. Lia turned to see if she could see who was humming, but it was too dim and the seat backs too close together. She thought of the woman in the back row, the book held to perfectly obscure her face.

Lia watched the couple diagonal to them, the young woman snapping her bracelet against her wrist. The young man sitting with her grabbed her wrist in a quick motion, tightened his grip, and Lia saw the young woman wince. In another couple, the grab might have seemed playful, light, in another couple.

One year, when they were at university, Lia had asked Lina why she had gone back to the country of their birth for school. She had expected Lina to say something about their roots, about exploring their past, and instead Lina had said, "God, weren't you just so tired of being the same person?" But, Lia had never thought of it like that, Lina was her best friend not her shadow. The words had echoed in her head for weeks, the exasperation and irritation in Lina's voice. All of Lia's childhood memories, the times they'd laid in bed and told secrets in the dark, the games where Lia always made sure Lina was with her all the way to the end, suddenly folded inwards. A castle of cards where only one wall was built.

The darkness of the plane got darker and a few people let out gasps. The line of safety lights had gone out. In the darkness, something moved. Walking up the aisle, but too low to the ground. Not walking. Someone crawled up the aisle. Lia heard the woman next to her, Sara, pull in a sharp breath of air. The light came back on and Lia looked to the aisle but nothing was there. Her seatmate was staring as well.

"Did you hear that?" Sara asked.

"It sounded like something in the aisle."

Sara nodded, her eyes still fixed to the airplane carpet. But there was nothing there.

The captain came on the overhead, "still a little bumpy out there, folks. I hear there was a light mishap as well. It should be smooth sailing soon."

Lia wondered if pilots ever panicked. If when a plane was going down they told everyone to pray, to think of their loved ones, to say goodbye to the earth as it reached up to hold them?

"Did you see the coffin being put into the plane?" Sara asked.

"I did, yeah."

"I asked and someone said it was a woman who had been murdered. You might have heard in the news, she was a tourist. They're returning her body home."

Lia had never paid much attention to the news, didn't know about the tourist. What must it have been like to be killed so far from home, from the people who loved you? "I didn't hear about that, no."

"Poor lady. Definitely feels ominous, huh? To be on a plane with a body."

Lia shrugged. They were returning the body home, which meant the woman was from the same place as Lia. Lia no longer thought of it as home, though, too many years in another country, another citizenship. Any traces of her accent long absorbed. She had been so young. Lina had gotten hers back, when they spoke on the phone she had the lilting arches of vowels that their mother still retained as well. *Your voice sounds so harsh,* Lina had said to Lia on one of their calls.

The humming restarted from behind their row, and Lia turned again in the dim to look. If she bent her head enough she could see slightly through the crack between seats. A few rows back she saw someone was doing the same thing and peeking through the crack at her. She jolted slightly in surprise. And then the face and its eye was gone.

The light flicked out again. Fewer people gasped, assuaged by the pilot's previous soothing, but Lia's body tensed. Something moved forward in the aisle again. She heard the little girl in the aisle across whisper something to her father, "I'm scared."

"Shhhh…" the thing in the aisle responded. It was gentle and yet Lia almost screamed when she heard it.

It was beside their row. It was so dark. *Don't let it see you.* Lia held her breath, tried to steady any movement she was making. She heard the young woman diagonal from her let out a whimper of sound, and the line of blue lights flickered on a for a split second. Had Lia been looking anywhere else, the split second would have revealed nothing. But Lia was staring where the young couple was, had followed the sound of the whimper, and in the split second she saw it. A form that looked like a woman and not. All of her angles just slightly wrong, an arm that bent the wrong way, hair that spread out around her as if she were suspended underwater. Where her face should have been just emptiness. She was leaning down in front of the young man. Placing her emptiness directly in front of his face. Then the light flicked back off. Dark dark.

Then the overhead lights burst into brightness. Lia felt herself blinking against the light. She looked at the couple and the thing, the woman, was gone. But so was the young man. The young woman sat by herself, she was scrolling her phone, through photos of partying college students. Her posture revealed boredom, as if nothing had happened.

"Did you see that?" Lia asked Sara.

"What?" Sara asked.

"The thing in the aisle?"

Sara shook her head. "I only heard it."

Lia pointed at the young woman. "Was she with someone before? A guy?"

Sara looked where she was pointing. "Uh, I…I thought so? I can't remember."

When they were teens, Lia and Lina would always stay up late the night before the new year of school started. Lia would talk about her classes, the friends she missed. Lina would gossip about what people had done over the summer. The night before their senior year, she went to bed early. Said nothing to Lia. Lia looked back on it sometimes and wondered if that was the moment her and her sister had finally drifted apart. Lina spent weekends at her job, nights out with boyfriends. Her parents told her she needed to spend more time with family and Lina muttered, "I've seen you all too much."

Lia had always assumed her sister had just been hit with teenageness a little more than she had, that her sister would return to her when hormones cooled down. But they'd never again spent nights staying up to meet the sun. They'd never again whispered in the dark. She missed it often, missed the ability to reach out and touch her sister's arm, feel her suppressing a giggle in the dark as they joked about their teachers. *Aren't you just so tired of being the same person?* But then *I need your help Lia.* And Lia had forgotten the years between them, the silence, the irritation in her sister's voice. She was waiting at the threshold, ready to make sure her sister got home safe.

The plane lurched again. Turbulence. Lia looked over at Sara, again scrolling her phone. The young woman on her phone. The little girl was still clutching her stuffed animal. Had Lia simply been dreaming? She tried to turn in her seat to see who was in the last row. The woman with the book that covered her face wasn't there, though. In the bathroom, maybe. Switched seats.

She turned to Sara, "You said the coffin, it was a murdered woman?"

Sara startled from her phone. "Yeah, well…that's what someone said. The poor tourist."

"What did she look like?"

Sara shrugged. "I don't know. I only saw a photo in the news briefly. Dark hair. Pretty. She looked like those photos always do."

Lia raised an eyebrow. "Always do?"

"You know, all murdered women in the news. They always pick some candid photo, staring at the camera. They always look younger than they are and happier probably too. They're smiling for someone behind the lens. It's not candid, just captured."

A photograph of Lina from the year before had been sent to their family group chat. She was in a summer dress, her hair up, and she was smiling at the camera. She looked different than Lia pictured her in her memory, like she was wearing someone else's style for a day. Lia had wondered who had taken the photo. A boyfriend? A friend? Some stranger on the street? Lia hadn't asked, her sister's short replies to questions, her ignoring any she didn't want to answer, had sat in Lia's head like a block as her hand hesitated over the phone keyboard. She'd replied, *nice photo! You look great!*

The lights flickered. The pilot's voice was a wave of calm: "We'll be out of this patchy area very soon, everyone. Skies are bright at our destination!"

Outside the sky was still just black. Lia pressed her face to the window, stared hard to see any bit of light from below. Nothing. As she pulled her face back, a reflection of someone standing in the aisle staring at her. She spun her head but no one was there.

The light went out.

Something coming up the aisle. Lia held her breath. A dark shape, somehow darker than the darkness of the plane which made it more visible, like someone had cut a patch out of the world and let the night shine through. Almost a woman's shape, but not. She leaned over Sara, who shook with fear. She placed her face, the absence of it, directly in front of Sara's.

"Oh, god, I see everything," Sara whispered.

The light turned on. Sara's seat was empty. There was no sign she had been there. No clothes, no bag under the seat in front of her. Just an empty seat. Lia felt herself shivering hard. She rang the bell for the flight attendant.

A cheerful woman walked up the aisle and bent down to Lia. "How can I help, Miss?"

Lia didn't know what to say, but her voice shook as she spoke. "The woman seated next to me. Do you know where she's gone?"

The flight attendant screwed her face into one of confusion. "This is an empty seat, ma'am? Did someone switch to sit near you? Maybe they've gone back to their designated seat."

"Oh, okay, maybe I'm, maybe I'm confused. Sorry to bother you." Lia looked around at the empty seats on the plane. More than she'd noticed before. She'd sworn it had been a full flight.

Why hadn't she told their parents that she was going to get Lina? She hadn't wanted to worry them, or maybe she'd just thought she'd handle it herself. She was her sister's keeper, she could keep her safe without their help. She wondered what they'd do if she didn't come back. Veronica would have to call them, say Lia was in a plane crash. She's gone. And they'd not understand why was she on a plane. Where was she going. Why hadn't she told them. Would they feel guilty? Would they think she hadn't trusted them? What else was she keeping from them?

Someone sat down next to Lia. She turned as the light went out.

The woman's shape turned to her. The emptiness of her face, unknowable. There were no emotions in the blank. Lia stilled her breath. *We need to get home before dark.* But there was nowhere to hide, no ducking and rolling from sight. The shape placed her face closer to Lia's, eye to the absence. Lia saw:

Nothing.

The shape pulled back. Cocked her head slightly. The light came back on. Lia sat shaking, but still in her seat. She looked over at the little girl and the little girl looked back at her. Smiled, like she might at a younger sibling to tell them they were okay.

Lia looked out the window and saw a city lighting up the ground in the distance.

"We've made it through the clouds, and it should be smooth sailing from here on out," the pilot said. The seatbelt sign flicked off. "Feel free to move about the cabin."

When the plane eventually landed, Lia messaged Lina. *Just landed. Tell me where to find you.* She waited for a response. Nothing. As she deboarded the plane, she kept her phone in her hand. Waiting for the buzz, the relief of an answer. She wondered what she'd tell Lina, if she'd say what had happened on the flight. What had happened on the flight? She bumped into the young woman on the gangway. "Sorry, I feel all turned around," the woman said. She looked slightly dazed, as if woken from a dream. On her wrist, a bruise below her bracelet. The shape of someone's hand grabbing her. Lia startled at the sight.

"No…no worries," she said to the woman. The flood of people spread out to their gates, to baggage, to their next stops. All on with their lives again. Lia wondered what stories about the flight they'd tell to the people they loved.

In her hand, the phone buzzed. An answer.

Variable Stars

If you go to the seashore and wait long enough, watching the waves come in and out, in and out, eventually the sun will start to dip and you'll see all the boats, the trawlers in the distance, turn their lights on one by one. It's like they are mirroring the stars popping into clarity in the darkening sky. If you wait long enough the sounds of the city disappear, the cars and honks and rush, and soon it's just the waves and the breeze and the lights in the distance. This is one of my favorite memories that I've walked inside, the woman with me just wanted to sit on the sand and watch the water. We sat there for hours, even though she knew that the longer we stayed, the more that she'd pay. Once she pointed out a shooting star, it was the first she'd spoken in at least an hour, and she said, "I made a wish on that one then, too." I wondered what her wish had been the first time and what it was now.

I didn't really know what Perfect Memory™ was when I first got hired. Time travel was a relatively new reality, mostly theoretical, and so heavily regulated by the government that I didn't even know any businesses could use it yet. I was fresh out of grad school with a degree in therapeutic art that I wasn't really sure how to transition into an actual career, and so when I saw a job posting looking for an "empathetic creative," I figured why not apply.

At the interview, they told me that they were looking for someone who could act as a guide without passing judgment. It sounded like nonsense, honestly, but I nodded and talked about a summer I'd spent as a volunteer tour guide at a local park. At the end of the interview, they asked me what my most perfect memory was. If I could return to just one moment in my life, which would it be. The question caught me off guard, and I said, "I don't know. I never really thought about it." And the woman doing the interview smiled.

I was hired the next day. Perfect Memory™ was highly organized and specific time travel for people that knew they couldn't change anything about the past. Not exactly tourism, there was no visiting dinosaurs or preventing the Lincoln assassination, as the science couldn't even go back further than fifty years, and you could only go someplace you'd already been once. I never really knew how it worked, and didn't understand enough to ask the right questions if they had been willing to tell me. Essentially, they could take someone back to their one perfect memory. The customer would tell them the rough time and place and they'd be sent back with a Perfect Guide™. That was me. Someone who would ensure that they didn't do anything to change the past, didn't interact with themselves, and that they had someone to talk to as they processed their emotions.

They could stay as long as they liked, but were charged by the hour, so most people chose an hour time frame. The first person I went back with was a man looking to return to a memory from his daughter's childhood.

It was a birthday party at one of those places designed specifically as torture for parents: loud gaming machines, bright lights, a furry mascot who took smoke breaks every three hours as was their right, and food that cost twice as much as the store-bought frozen version but tasted half as good. I'd only ever done memory leaps in training, and the feeling was still new to me. A rush in the tummy like when you're heading up a drop on a rollercoaster, then a slight blur of vision, and then you'd be at your targeted site with the Perfect Memory™ bracelet tingling at your wrist.

We watched the man's daughter race around the building, other children screaming with joy alongside her. I saw the woman who must have been her mother, looking frazzled as she kept an eye on everything. Then I saw our client, twenty-ish years younger but recognizable still. He was on his phone, constantly. Either checking emails or occasionally taking calls, he'd stalk outside holding the phone with voice raised to be heard above the din.

"I couldn't even give her two hours," the man said from beside me.

I turned to him, watched him watching his daughter. "She still looks happy. It was a good birthday."

"She never needed me there to be happy," he said.

We stayed only thirty minutes or so, and then he was ready to go home. I had to ask him, "This is your perfect memory?"

"It's the one I was there for the most, in all honesty." He said and shook his head.

Most people weren't so self-aware about their memories, though.

There was a woman who wanted to go back to a picnic as a child, and her parents glared at each other the whole time. There was a man who took us back to the perfect date he'd had with the woman he called his one true love, and the entire time you could see her having fun in the moment but looking at every other man that passed by as if wondering how easy it would be to slip inside the life of someone else. There were the people that wanted to see their proposals, the moment they met someone, and they were filled with texting other people, nodding along to jokes without laughing. There was so much wastefulness of time in everyone's memories.

Everyone who left Perfect Memory™ rated their satisfaction as a ten out of ten. They paid their fees. None of them wanted to admit that they'd paid so much to not be happy with the outcome. One of the other Perfect Guides™ looked at me one day as a client left and said, "It's a great business, isn't it?"

"Is it?"

"Yeah, because they're going to come back and look at another memory. They're going to keep doing that thinking the next memory will actually be perfect."

"Do you think everyone has such bad memory of the past?"

She shrugged, "It's not a bad memory. It's just none of us know a perfect memory, right? Like think about it, we remember these big events. The things we think were a moment of change—we fell in love, we got married, we had a kid. But those aren't the ones we'd curl up inside of, not really."

"Where would you go?" I asked and she looked over at me all conspiratorially.

"Back to Paris. I went there on my honeymoon. We've divorced, it was certainly not a perfect memory. But there was a croissant I'd kill to have again."

I laughed, but I didn't believe her.

One guy took us to a darkened street outside of his childhood home. It must have been winter, because it had a deep chill, and I watched my breath curl out of my mouth as we stood outside.

We just stared at the house, but didn't go close, didn't peek in any windows.

We only stayed fifteen minutes or so, I could see the cold settling in him as he said we should go. I wanted to ask what the memory was, what he'd wanted to see, but it was my job to know when to ask and when not to. When we got back to the Perfect Memory™ headquarters, he rubbed his arms to erase the last bit of cold, and nodded at me as he went to pay. Just a middle-aged man, who had wanted to watch a quiet house in the dark.

Not all jobs last forever. The money was good, and the work was easy enough, but I started to hear rumors of government interference eventually. They had begun to lock down on unregulated time travel, bills were being written to ensure it could only be done for scientific or government purposes. I wondered how soon it would be before our pasts started to get rewritten without us even knowing about it. But it wasn't there yet, we all had time and other worries.

When Perfect Memory™ said they were shutting down, they gave us what my colleagues called a "handsome" severance of a quarter of a year. I figured I'd use the money to figure out my life. It was good to have time. On my last day, the lady who had been in my hiring interview asked me if I'd miss the job.

"I will," I said. But it wasn't exactly the truth. I'd miss the pay and the ease of it, I'd miss the window into other lives, but I wouldn't miss seeing everyone, over and over, realize that their pasts weren't beautiful.

"Did you ever think of a memory?" she asked.

I shook my head.

"Yeah, I never did either. Maybe I'll make one someday."

It's been years since I worked there. And I don't think about it often, but when I do, I'll usually end up driving somewhere nice—a seashore, a forest, a café that lets you sit a long time—and I'll try to remember every detail around me. I'll sit and sit and wonder who else will remember this moment.

Other Vertigos

Clarissa felt things begin to spin around her. It was a slight sensation, at first, a feeling of something being off in a miniscule way, like a tremble on the surface of a glass of water.

In the Out, it's hard to realize the difference between truly feeling things spinning and a false sensation of dizziness. People who had been on the station a long time called it the "Spins." Clarissa had never had the Spins before. Not even during her training, where people sometimes got it so bad that they ended up never going into space at all. This had even happened to her own sister. Clarissa often thought of her sister's face after finding out she couldn't go into space, the way her eyes seemed even to dull. And then Clarissa had gone, and when they spoke, they spoke of anything other than their careers. They spun large circles around the topic.

Spinning. Was it spinning?

The thing was that a person needed to be able to make that differentiation almost instantaneously. If the actual station, or pod, or ship, if that's where the person was, was actually spinning, then something was very wrong. It could be any number of things, but all of those things needed to be acted on quickly to avoid disaster. And disaster in the Out was not something to be taken lightly.

She wasn't far from the station. The pod was on a routine loop. She'd done it dozens of times before. Closing her eyes, Clarissa tried to focus on the feeling. Was it in her feet? Her vision? Still there.

There were steps to this: keep calm, check surroundings, analyze. Taking a breath in and out, Clarissa opened her eyes. She touched the sides of the pod and felt vibrations. Not the normal thrumming feeling, that was a pleasant one like a kitten's purrs; this was a rumble, more like a lion's growl.

Don't panic. Keep calm. It had happened once before. Clarissa had heard about a pod, with a minuscule crack along the outside that the station mechanics had never noticed, splitting open during a loop, *like a pineapple hit by a machete* was the phrase Clarissa had heard bandied about.

The control panel was in front of her. She pressed the emergency button. The station would tell her what to do. She had always trusted in the station.

"What's the matter?" A man's voice. Amber looked up at him. He seemed so tall. "Miss, are you okay?"

She was on the ground. Amber remembered being on a run, the pleasant pounding feel of the dirt path beneath her feet. Sitting up, she felt her head gingerly with the tips of her fingers. No bumps. No blood. "I must have fallen."

The man reached down, holding out a hand. She took it and he helped her to her feet. She felt dizzy, like everything was spinning.

"Do you need some water? It's pretty hot out, you could be dehydrated," the man said. It sounded reasonable enough.

Amber pulled out her own water bottle from her waist pouch, smiled at the man to show she was fine. He nodded at her, then continued his jog. Taking a swig of water, the spinning intensified for a moment.

She'd had dizzy spells as a child, something to do with her inner ears. There had been a surgery to correct it. Years later, though, it had been the medical team's reason for not letting her go into the Out.

"You need to be able to tell, Amber, if there is something wrong at all times. We can't chance that you'll think you're just experiencing vertigo."

"I won't. Please, I won't." Her voice had come out whiny, begging. For a second, she'd hated herself. Her sister had been the one, then, who ended up going into the Out. Solid Clarissa, who never even thought about the movement of the Earth beneath her feet.

Beginning to run again, she'd shake it off. The world would still itself.

Many astronauts felt vertigo trying to land their spacecraft— a feeling of heaviness in the limbs and lightness in the head. Troy had heard it explained to him more than once. The key was to focus on something small and steady.

He dreamed, often, of the landing. The way the surface had come up towards him too fast. He'd braced for impact. The body has an exceptional ability to prepare for the worst, even as one can't mentally comprehend what's happening.

His co-pilot hadn't been as lucky. An accident. It shouldn't have happened. The medical team explained that it wasn't Troy's fault. He'd taken a year of medical leave and there had been a long series of tests before he was allowed to come back. You have to believe that you're ready to come back, that's what one of the pamphlets said.

He tried hard to believe it. Sometimes, though, he'd see something out of the corner of his eyes. A person spinning in place, a cup turning as if on a record player. Things that shouldn't be moving. He wasn't a pilot anymore. Maybe that made it alright that he was never sure.

"Please repeat your situation," he said into the mic.

"I feel spinning. And there's a, a vibration, a hard one, in the side of my pod," the woman said. She had stated her name, and pod name, but he already couldn't remember it.

"How long have you been feeling this?" Troy asked. There was a protocol.

"The past, uh, maybe, five minutes?" The woman's voice had the slightest shake, her breath wavering as if she was beginning to shiver.

Troy pulled up a vid screen. He was able to get the pod in sight and then had to hold in a gasp. The crack on the pod's side looked like someone had taken a gigantic permanent marker and drawn a line all around. There were maybe only minutes before it split. There was nothing anyone could do. There was nothing.

"You're looking fine. Maybe it's the spins?" he said. It was likely that she wouldn't even feel anything. The split would happen in an instant, and she really might not feel anything.

Amber found a bench and sat down. The feeling still there. The blue sky, even, seemed to be spiraling around her. If it hadn't felt so disconcerting, it might have been pretty to behold. Leaning over, she pressed a hand to each side of her face. She breathed in and out. In and out.

"One. Two. Three. Four." Her doctors had told her as a child that she should count herself back to serenity. It had worked as a child: when she reached ten, she'd always felt the spinning go away.

Clarissa heard something in the voice on the monitor. He was trying to be kind. The spinning was everywhere. It climbed her legs, played at the base of her skull. She sat down as the vibrations became stronger.

As a child, her older sister had loved to grab Clarissa by the arms and spin her in circles. Amber said she was letting Clarissa feel what her world was like. Spinning her faster and faster. Clarissa would giggle and scream. The dizzy feeling staying long after they'd spun themselves into exhaustion.

"Count to ten," her sister would say. "You'll feel better when you get to ten."

"One. Two. Three. Four. Five. Six. Seven." Clarissa began.

Troy wanted to look away. He'd called the necessary people. Alerted any other pods in the direct vicinity. He'd heard of what they looked like when they cracked open. All of the pressure of space at once. He didn't look away. Someone needed to see it and know that there had been a loss.

"Jesus," he whispered as the pod blossomed open.

"Nine. Ten," Amber said. Raising her head, the world felt itself again. She looked up at the sky and for a second it seemed even brighter than it had before. Then it was fine, normal again. She stood up and headed home. The world was calm beneath her feet.

A Path of Needles

Girls went missing all the time in the city. Sometimes in groups of two or three on their ways to parties or headed to the store because a mother told them to remember milk on their way home, but most often alone. All alone.

Hannah Grossi wore her hair in a French braid. She could never do them herself and so her sister had helped her—brushing her hair out first until it seemed to glow. Hannah admired the braid in the mirror before going out.

The mall in the city had been so busy. She kept running into people she knew. It was the first time, in quite a while that she'd gone out by herself. The people were so overwhelming.

Hannah wanted to call her sister, have her come to get her. Then Hannah ran into Tara Ross. Tara Ross, with her bubblegum pink hair and bright makeup. Tara Ross who would remember Hannah a couple of years later, as she woke up in a hospital bed after a mistake—at least, that's what she'd tell the hospital psych team—that she'd never make again, and would realize that she'd never quite forget Hannah. Never quite forget that moment.

Tara Ross gently tugged down Hannah's sleeve before Hannah could stop her. "Shit, you're gonna never be able to cover those up."

Hannah had pulled away, yanking her sleeve down to cover the still raggedly red scar tissue. She'd pushed away through the crowds, so many people pushing in around her.

Outside, the air felt so crisp and cool, and she had trouble pulling in each breath. She'd just go home. The forest was a shortcut. She started down the path.

Inside the woods, it was so quiet. Hannah reached into her pocket, felt her phone, thought of still calling her sister.

"Hello," someone said. A person on the path, not far in front of her. The person was covered in shadows. But it wasn't that dark, Hannah thought.

"Uh, hi," Hannah said.

In the trees, a bird started singing. So low and deep. Deeper than any birdsong she'd ever heard.

"You're afraid of the dark," the person said. Somehow, they were standing next to Hannah.

And she was. The dark and the party and the boy she didn't know. Hannah had tried to get away then, too. Hannah's phone rang, the vibration against her hand felt like when the train roared past her house when she was trying to sleep. But, it was too late to answer and Hannah heard birds singing, and only as the phone stopped ringing did she realize that the song was her.

Maura came to the city after her sister Maria called her to say that girls were disappearing in droves. Only her sister had said, "Girls are, like, disappearing in doves, Maura." And Maura had imagined that there were girls climbing into giant doves all over the city and then not coming back out.

Maura's sister was a college student in the city. She studied interior design, how to make enjoyable spaces, as she explained it. So you're not just in a house, you're in your home, was her motto. Maura's home, hours and hours from the city, was simple and the walls were unpainted and that was the way she liked it. Rooms with four walls and no weird angles.

"You're here!" Maria exclaimed when she swung open the door, following Maura's light knock.

Maura nodded and stepped inside the apartment. It had first apartment written all over it: A kitchen the size of a closet and bean bag chairs everywhere. Maria's roommate was an art student named Greta. Maura often overheard her during phone calls extolling how the light looked or how the color of an avocado was just so abstract.

"So girls are disappearing?" Maura asked. She liked getting down to things.

"Like so many girls!" Maria shouted. She raised her arms up, spreading her palms out, as if to encompass just how many girls it was.

"How long has it been happening?" Maura asked, looking around for a place to sit. The bean bag chairs didn't seem promising.

"Months, but more and more recently," Maria said.

"And what have the police said?" Maura asked. Giving up on sitting, she leaned against the wall.

"You know, you know, what they always say."

And Maura did know. The police always said: We have no new leads, the public should not be worried, the girls were out late, the girls shouldn't have been talking to strangers. Or maybe, they just implied some of those things. Maura remembered when Indira disappeared. The police had talked to Maura for hours, feeling like days, had asked her if maybe Indira had just found someone else, someone her parents may have found more suitable. They never said "man," but Maura heard it behind every word. Indira's parents had loved Maura, had made her cups of tea when she visited, and sometimes Indira's mother still called her up, and they would share stories back and forth about Indira. The moments the other had never gotten to see: Indira's mother would tell her about tiny Indira playing in the snow, and Maura would tell her about how Indira braided her hair after the shower, the quick deftness of her fingers as if she wasn't even thinking about the braid at all.

"And what is the gossip?" Maura asked.

"Oh, everyone has different theories. The best was Aliens, the worst was Serial Killer."

Maria moved into the kitchen, so Maura leaned upwards from the wall and followed her. "What do you think, Maria?"

Maria shrugged, opening the fridge door and pulling out a bottle of sparkling water. "They're all young. They mostly disappear alone. That's why I called you."

Maura watched Maria struggle to open the bottle. She'd never had a strong grip. As children, Maura always opened everything for her. Their mother would sigh, "Let her do it herself, Maura or she'll never be able to do it."

Maura took the bottle from her, twisting the cap off with ease. "I don't do that anymore, Maria."

"Why not? It's your gift," Maria said.

"A gift?" Maura responded. She thought of her childhood, the sharp turn of her body when a girl needed her. It had always seemed a curse.

They'd discovered her power when Lucy Albertson, age seven, never came home from school one day. Maura, age four, sat in a tree, and her body had suddenly wrenched to the right. And then she fell, body twisting in the air. She felt like a maple key turning with the wind. Landing on the ground, her body pointed due east. The fall hadn't hurt, not even knocked the wind out, and so she stood up and walked in the direction her body told her. It was into the woods, McCarthy's place, where her parents always told her not to go. She walked and walked and walked until she found Lucy. Lucy had passed out at some point from pain or blood loss. Her leg was clamped tight in a coyote trap.

Years later, Maura would sometimes spill a glass of wine down the sink, and the swirl of red would make her queasy, reminding her of a little girl with her bright yellow pants stained darkly maroon.

Lucy lived, though her leg didn't. At first, everyone praised Maura, though her mother also yelled at her for wandering off, but then another girl went missing. Amber Halloway, sixteen, and everyone's favorite cashier at the Pig. Maura found her body in the middle of the night, having sleepwalked to the spot, her body directed as skillfully as a marionette. Amber Halloway had been killed. Maura's mother took to locking her in her bedroom at night. "This might be a gift, but you don't need to use it."

And Maura rarely did when she was a child. She used it more as a teen. Sneaking out at night, climbing down the trellis by her window, to find friends who'd had a drink too many, who were climbing into the cars of boys they shouldn't, and Maura would be there. She liked those ones best—the just about missing. Those were the only times when it felt like it might truly have been a gift.

"It is a gift," Maria insisted.

Maura sighed. "But, I don't do that anymore."

Maria took a sip of her water, swishing it in her mouth for a long moment. "I know. But please?"

Maura nodded, though even that small an acknowledgement felt like slipping off the edge of something.

In the dark of the room, Indira sat at the edge of the bed. Her face hidden in shadows. Maura pretended to still be asleep. The vision always left when she was fully awake. Indira was drawing something. A pad of paper in her hand. Indira's hair was the shade of the night. How many times had Maura gone through color catalogues trying to find that exact kind of darkness and not been able to?

Maura couldn't help herself. She reached out and her hand touched the nothing that was there. Indira faded.

Maura's gift had only not worked once. The one time she would've given anything for it to have. She had thought about that. What it might mean. Maybe Indira was beyond missing. She was gone, gone, gone, as if she'd never existed. Excised. Erased. Even the police stopped caring; wouldn't take Maura's calls after a certain point. Eradicated.

Maura turned on the light. The hotel room was tiny, uncomfortably not her own. She wondered if Maria was up. If another girl was already missing.

Maura stepped out of bed and went to the window. The city shone with the rising sun. The glass in windows sparkled. The street below slowly came to life. Maura's gaze fell on the forest at the city's heart. It looked like it didn't belong exactly, like someone had transplanted it out of the realm of faery and no one had noticed. As Maura stared, she barely noticed as her body leaned forward, pressing against the window. Her fingers undid the latch, as if of their own volition, and the window swung out, and she swung out with it.

"Shit!" Maura yelped. Luckily, the window's safety hinge locked into place, leaving only a six-inch gap open, and so Maura didn't fall.

Maura slowed her breathing back down, felt her heart returning from its exaggerated pace. Her arm raised, her fingers bending on their own, so forcefully that her fingernails dug into her palm painfully. Only her index finger remained out— pointing at the forest.

It was a Tuesday and raining. They met waiting for a bus. Maura usually took the earlier one, but had been lost in a daydream and missed it. She didn't have an umbrella. Her hair was drenched. Then she saw a woman, dressed in yellow galoshes, spinning a pink umbrella. The woman saw her, hair the color of the sky removed of stars if that could be beautiful, and motioned to her to come hide from the rain with her.

And then it had been a Saturday, years later, and hot outside. And Indira had gotten called into work. She'd kissed Maura once goodbye, sighing at the heat as she swung the door open. Maura hadn't been watching her leave, had already turned, but she'd turned around when the door closed. There was a feeling in her throat like she was about to cry though she didn't know why. Often, she'd come back to that. There were so many warnings in life that people never paid attention to.

Maura stepped into the forest. She had called her sister once, said what she was doing, but not where she was going. Maria was the kind of girl who ran in before calling the police. Maura didn't need headstrong and foolish.

The path was winding. The trees dense.

She walked and walked and walked. The forest seemed unending. The light from outside the trees was dull, distant.

"Hello," someone said. A person standing on the side of the path. Not necessarily a man or woman. Just a shape like a person. Their face was completely obscured in shadow.

"Hello," Maura said. Her body turned to stare at the person full on, though Maura had not meant to turn. So this, then, was her answer. "Who are you?"

"I am…" The person shrugged. "Who are you?"

"What are you?" Maura asked. Asking the right questions was always important.

The person chuckled, deep and unsettling. "I'm the path."

"To what?"

It shrugged again.

"What do you do to them?" Maura asked. "Where are the girls?"

"Gone. I take away their fear. I eat it all up. I'm…Helpful," It said, sounding pleased to explain itself.

"Fear?"

"Girls are so full of them, you know. They're gorged with fears. Fear of being ashamed, of being called names. Petty fears." It laughed again and Maura felt her hands curling into fists. "Best of all, they're all afraid of the dark."

It stepped closer to Maura. So like a person, but not. Like someone's imagining of a person.

"Who are you to call them petty?" Maura asked.

"I'm not afraid," it said, as if that were answer enough. "I'm not afraid of the dark."

It was right next to Maura.

"I'm not afraid of the dark, either," Maura said.

"Everyone is," It said, opening Its mouth. Around them, birds began to sing, hopping on tree branches. They were calling out a warning, Maura understood.

But it wasn't true. In the dark, Indira came back to Maura. In the night, drained of any light, she saw Indira's hair spread across a pillow. Maura begged for the dark some nights.

Its mouth was like a black hole, filled with the caught screams of so many women. Maura reached into Its mouth, down Its throat and grabbed at the darkness. It struggled, surprised. Maura pulled at something. She felt a swell of something inside her, her whole body fought on her side, and she wondered if it was rage she was feeling. Or if it was grief.

It started to shriek and Its screams made It sound so afraid. Maura pulled and pulled and It began to unravel. Spools of darkness flickering out into the air. Maura felt her strength giving out and still she pulled. The trees were fading around her. The birds were singing louder.

At last, the person-who-was-no-person was completely gone. The forest itself was gone. There was just a stone in Maura's hands—black and dull. A rock that no one would've picked up from the ground.

Maura fell onto the earth. A bird landed next to her, followed by another and another until a hundred birds had surrounded her. One hopped onto her hand and tugged loose the rock. Then the birds began to peck at it until even that was gone. Obliterated. The birds rose into the air, singing. This time their song sounded mournful, but not without beauty, not without hope.

Maura got to her feet. Her whole body ached. She wondered what her sister was doing. Perhaps, over dinner, Maura might tell her what she'd seen. Or, maybe, she'd just say it was over.

That night, Maura woke in her darkened hotel room. Indira sat on her bed. Maura said something she'd never said before, a single word. A word she hoped would help Indira move on. And then there was no one there, just the song of some night bird outside the window—feathers as dark as loss itself.

Boy and Cave and Man and Night

At eight o'clock on a Saturday night, the sky opens up so subtly that no one will notice for a few more hours. It's just a splash of extra-dark across the night, some stars excised, but they'd been dead for years anyway. When Alex notices it, he thinks it is a floater in his vision, just a trick of pain.

An eye doctor once told him that migraines were the leading cause of strokes in young people. And Alex had said, "What can I do about them?" And the doctor had shrugged. When Alex's sees the hole in the sky, he blinks, shifts his eyes to look somewhere else. But the extra-dark is still there. He covers one eye with a hand and then the other.

Once, when he was a child, he climbed into a cave on his parents' land. It was in the woods behind the house, set into the side of a bluff. The opening was wide, and he thought maybe something cool lived there. A bear or a badger. And he was young enough to think running into one would be cool and not scary. He hadn't yet learned that nature could hold the edge of its blade to your throat. He climbed into the cave and realized the ceiling was low enough that he needed to crawl, so he got on his knees and started to move forward into the dark. He didn't notice the earth growing narrower and narrower around him. Not until the bright sun from outside was almost gone, and he was in darkness, and the cold of the earth was so close to him.

And he was in darkness.

Alex watches the sky, and it watches him, as skies so often do. It opens more, a subtle shift that wipes away galaxies, but that Alex registers as a mouth opening just a little wider than it should. He thinks to call someone, ask them if they see it too, if it's just a migraine, or if there really is something wrong with the night. But his phone is in his backpack, and he doesn't want to take his eyes off the night.

In the cave, there was only dark ahead and he couldn't see the light behind him. He started to crawl back, but in his panic, in the ground, in the scrunching up of his clothes as he crawled, he realized he was stuck.

And who would he call? He's walking home after work, a shift that ran long and then longer still, until his feet ached and his back ached and he wondered what would happen if he just went home and slept for days. He'd call his mother, but the home turned off her phone after dinner. He'd call his brother, but his brother hasn't picked up in years, hasn't been alive in years. His photo is on a memorial wall somewhere, but Alex never went to see it. He'd call.

In the cave, he yelled out for his father. Yelled and yelled. But he knew, he just knew, that no one could hear him. He was tucked inside the dark, inside the earth, like when a snake swallowed something whole and you couldn't hear it once it was inside that scaled belly. He didn't want to panic, but he felt it all over him, that creep of dread. Like he'd once watched his closet door slowly swing open one night, and he was so scared, so sure that something bad was in his closet, was about to come out to see him. But there was only the dark, the empty.

And the opening of the sky was so empty, so filled with absence, that it was blanker space even than his floaters. No light, no sense of something he was missing. It was just the sky opening up into before it ever existed. There is no knowing what came before the universe, just the believing that there had to be something. Alex stared and saw stars disappear, saw everything returning to blankness.

In the cave, he'd closed his eyes. He'd listened to his heart beating. So hard and fast, boots stomping against the ground. He'd begun to inch back, slow, slow, easy. Kept his eyes closed, as tight as he could, until he opened them and there was light again. He felt the earth opening out around him.

He thinks I should call someone. Someone else should see this. But he doesn't reach for his phone. It's all so close. He could just reach out and touch the absence. What is it like to feel an undoing, he wonders.

But he doesn't wonder for long.

The Dead We Carry Like Leaves

This is my war story. Way down there in the dark, the memory flickers like shooting stars. Just rocks burning through the atmosphere.

I never looked at the stars when I was on the front. Not even on quiet nights, when we were nowhere near battle and the air held a hush that meant everything was going to be alright—at least for a moment, at least for the night. At home, the stars used to be my favorite thing. I'd lie on the grass of my backyard and stare at them for hours, until my body was tired enough that I could go inside and fall easily into sleep. Maybe on the front, I never wanted to rest soundly.

Caleb told me all about the stars, though. While we were pacing back and forth on a night shift, he brought them up with the ease of someone who actually enjoyed conversation for the sake of it. I never thought Caleb had an end game in his words. He just liked engaging with someone else, taking the quiet from the air for a little bit.

"Damn, do you ever just look up and think how many other places there must be out there?" He stared up at the night as he spoke.

"Other places? Like planets, you mean?" I stared at the ground as I spoke, the dirt so dark that it could have been a starless sky itself.

"Yeah, planets. But also like places. Like cities and towns, and cafes. Places we might have wanted to go, if we lived there." He nodded his head once, an affirmation of something. "I watched a documentary on that once. All the chances that there are other planets with civilizations like ours. There could be hundreds of them, thousands really."

"I've heard that," I said. I never wanted to give out my personal history to the others; we were connected enough as it was, but Caleb was sweet and a kid, and I felt for his want of connection. "My husband's an astrophysicist. That's what he works on and does and thinks about all the time. Those possibilities out there."

Caleb turned to me, his smile shining in the minimal lights we kept with us on patrol. "Does he think we'll ever find some other place?"

I don't remember how I answered. If I tried to sound hopeful or if I made a joke or if I let the truth slip out of my mouth— how I hoped we'd never find somewhere else. The next morning was when the attack came, and everything went upside down.

Eating a breakfast ration, while Doreen went through a list of things she'd want to tell her son back home the next time she vidcalled with him, I thought about where we were at in the war. It had been three years since we first stationed troops there, and the progress we had made seemed so small as to seem nonexistent. My husband sometimes talked about the way that the news portrayed it back home. *Not at all,* is what he'd say. *They haven't talked about the war in a year.* It was an exaggeration on his part, of course. They always mentioned when someone died. A quick blip of a name and an age. Local news stations covered the stories more, of course. There'd be memorials, interviews with the family, an old friend who popped out of the woodwork to say: He/she/they was the kindest/most honest/truest soul I ever met.

"I want to tell him about the sound of the birds here," Doreen said to no one in particular. "Someone remind me. That ta-weet sound. Brody likes birds. He'll know what kind they are, I bet."

"I hate birds," Ariel said. I hadn't even seen him walk in, but he was already slumped in a chair somehow.

"How can you hate birds?" Van asked.

"Noisy fucks. That's how."

I kept thinking about the front, about the battles, about how we stayed stationed here despite the whole place seeming quiet.

People went about their days as if their city wasn't filled with our loud boots and vehicles, as if we weren't walking around with guns the size of toddlers in our arms. I'd seen a woman and her daughters walk past us the other day, and one of the daughters had bumped right into a soldier; she just adjusted her direction and kept walking, without even a second glance. It was like we were statues, things that had always been part of the scenery. I wondered sometimes if at home they talked about us, if their voices dipped into whispers about when we'd leave, if we'd ever leave, if their home would ever feel like their home again.

"Ta-weet, ta-weet. More like shut the fuck up."

Outside, the winds were picking up. They moaned and roared. I could hear the birds too, all of a sudden. The rising cries and chirps. So much sound.

"Shit," I said. But no one heard me through the sound of the explosion.

I opened my eyes to dust and smoke. My ears were ringing so loud that I couldn't hear anything else, except the thud-thud of my heart underneath it all. I couldn't breathe, all the air sucked out of my lungs like when I used to fall off swings as a kid, I only ever fell when I was on the highest point of the arc, trying to flip myself over the bars. I remembered: swing, sun, air, fall. Swing, sun, air, fall. Then I coughed and was able to pull in a sharp breath.

I was on my back, but not hurt other than the wind had been knocked out of me. I scrabbled over onto my knees, checked my gun where it sat snug against my hip, and crawled forward to where Doreen was. She stared up at the ceiling, but there was no light there. I gently removed her patch from behind her ear and slid it into the slot in my helmet, designed exactly for the purpose. I'd never had to do it before, though it was my position to do so—I was the Keeper for the unit. We'd never lost anyone before.

As the patch clicked into place, Doreen's voice flicked on. "Kendra?"

"Yes," I said. Voice scratchy from dust.

"Oh god. I was hoping I was dreaming. I saw birds, you know, when everything went dark. I saw birds."

"I'm sorry, Doreen," I said.

There was a long pause. "Get me home to my son. Promise?"

"I will," I said.

My husband, Evan, was against me being a Keeper when I was asked. I was trained as a medic, which made me think the higher-ups thought one empathetic field might as well be another.

"Do you understand what a Keeper has to do?" Evan asked.

"Better than you do, I'm sure." I'd always been fine with my husband over-explaining his work to me. I liked the careful way he broke it down for someone who didn't have his background of knowledge—the analogies and metaphors he'd use to guide me towards understanding. But, when it came to my career, I didn't like him taking the tone of superior knowledge.

"That's a weight, Kendra. It'll be such a weight."

I thought about everything I'd heard about Keepers. The way the patch worked---it carried a soldier's memories and their final "Presence," as it was called, until the patch could be returned to their family to be laid to rest. A Keeper's job was to keep the patches safe and to keep the Presences lucid for their final talk with their loved ones; they began to fade out after a while, unless they had someone to patch into.

"Then let's hope I'll never have to carry it." I had said. There must have been finality in my voice because Evan never brought it up again, though sometimes he'd sigh when he saw me practicing stealth maneuvers with artificial patches hooked up. It was hard to be silent, be smart, when you had more voices in your head than just your own.

"Doreen. Shit. Shit." Ariel knelt by her body longer than any of us. He turned to me, "Tell her I was just messing about the birds."

"She can hear you just fine, Ariel. As long as I can hear you."

He nodded. "Sorry, Doreen. I was just messing. I can like birds."

We studied each other, memorizing each other's faces, as Ariel stayed kneeling by the body.

Our CO, Taryn, didn't have any idea what was going on. "We're under attack. But it doesn't make sense."

Outside, I heard more explosions. When the next blast hit us, we were all already expecting it.

Bread baking smells like home. Home is where the heat is. No, the heart is. No home is where we are. We are not home.

This time: rubble. This devastation: complete. Then Taryn shaking me to full consciousness. "We need to get to Post 79. Get survivors there, and we can regroup and figure out what is going on."

Post 79 was a safe zone. Technically, breaching the peace there was considered a war crime. It was ten miles. I used my arms to push myself up from the ground and to my feet. Everything in my body pulsed with sharp pain. Around us, I saw rubble and bodies. Angie, Van, Blake. Each patch clicked into place, and I heard their voices echo in my head.

"Jesus, all of you?" Doreen asked.

"What happens now?" Angie asked.

"Kendra gets us home," Van said.

Blake stayed silent for long enough that I worried his patch hadn't worked, but then, finally, "Get us home, Kendra."

The first day of meeting our squad, they had me talk with everyone else one-on-one. It was a part of being a Keeper, your fellow soldiers needed to trust you, and you needed to know enough about them each that you could keep them threaded to their patch.

Blake had grown up on a farm in the country. His parents raised chickens and sold organic vegetables at farmers' markets. He said he had always wanted to get out and away. He hated that all of his neighbors knew him, would stop him to chat whenever he walked home from school.

"What do you think about that now?" I asked.

"Look, Kendra, I joined the military. It's literally just people endlessly stopping you to chat when they're bored on their shifts." He chuckled. "We all get so tangled in what we hate that we don't realize it's just life."

He had his parents, a little sister, and a girlfriend. Each of them vid-calling him to ask how he was once a week. He'd laugh, tell them stories, and his whole body came alive. Stories felt better to tell when everyone was so far away.

Of our squad, there were Taryn, Caleb, Ariel, and me. The other squad at our Outpost had been on patrol. Taryn had managed to get a radio through to them to tell them to go to 79. The radio fell into static as she was speaking. Then silence.

"Did they get the message?" Caleb asked, and he was bobbing on the heels of his feet. Nerves.

"I don't know. I think so." Taryn said.

Outside, the sky was dusky and dusty. We'd be in full dark soon, but it would be a boon as we tried to make it to 79. I'd been outside in the dark around the city often on patrols, and it was always quiet, peaceful. I'd look into houses as we passed, families curled up inside with lights out after curfew, and I'd wondered what everyone was dreaming inside. That night, though, the dark felt dangerous. The unlit houses could be hiding anything. The woods and better cover were only a couple of miles out. If we could make it to the woods, we'd have more opportunity to pass undetected from whoever had hit the outpost.

"Don't trust the woods," Blake said.

"Why?" Van said.

We never patrolled that far out. I asked him what he meant.

"I used to walk out there. Just so I could have a sense of trees. It's less cover than you think. Spooky out there. Stay on guard."

"It's plenty of cover," Van said. Sharper this time. "Don't overthink it, Kendra."

The city was silent. Then it wasn't. When the blast hit, it hit further from us than the sound would have made it seem. We all spun towards it. Saw a building torn into flames. It was the opposing outpost. We never really dealt with them.

"Is that fire from us?" Taryn asked. It took me a moment to realize that Us meant home, not actually us.

"It has to be, right?" Caleb said.

Taryn frowned. "We don't have any drones in this area."

Another explosion to our right. We all crouched instinctually, as if that would make a difference. Taryn motioned for us to move towards the end of the alleyway. We'd just need to make it through the alleys, then open space for half a mile, then the woods.

Once, when I was a child, my father had me walk the property lines with him. We'd come to a baby deer that had gotten caught in the fence. Tangled up, drooping over. I'd teared up, scared. My father had walked up to it, and the deer had startled, somehow still alive, just exhausted. My father had told me to go home and get his tool bag. I'd run as fast as I could. When I got back, I saw him crouched next to the deer. Its head was hanging low. But it was eating berries from his hand that he'd collected from a nearby blackcap bush.

He'd taken the wire cutter from his bag and carefully deconstructed the fence around the deer. Its legs too weak to keep it standing. He'd lifted it up and we'd slowly marched home, with him carrying the deer. With water and food, eventually it was able to stand.

"See that, Kendra," he pointed as the deer began to walk away from us.

"It's okay," I'd said.

"Miracles are just action and patience," he'd said.

The alleyway was darker somehow than the street had been. As if the shadows pulled any excess light into them. Taryn in lead, Ariel pulling up the rear. Caleb was ahead of me, and I could see his outline shaking. We were silent. Even the dead were silent in my head.

The shadows reached further out as we walked, the darkness catching at our feet. I heard the drone before we saw anything. The softest buzz, as if a hundred bees moved their wings in unison next to my ear.

"Down!" I shout-whispered.

We dropped to the ground as one, but like a building collapsing, Ariel fell last. Just a fraction of a second too long to fall. Whether his height or something else. I didn't hear the bullet firing, only the sharp intake of Ariel gasping as it hit him.

Ariel once on a patrol, tossing an orange between his hands as we walked. He'd spent a summer as a carnival worker, going town to town and helping erect rides and displays. He said he'd asked each performer to teach him one thing. He could juggle up to two objects, could breathe fire, knew how to always guess someone's weight correctly. The only one he'd ever shown off, though, was the juggling. Orange to hand, hand to orange, orange to hand.

He held his pain in his clenched teeth, even dying, he didn't want to betray our position. Blood ran through my hands as I tried to compress the wound. Caleb clutched his hand, and I wasn't sure if Caleb was trying to comfort Ariel or himself.

"Kendra, tell my mom, tell her—" he said. And then he was gone. I took his patch and clicked it into place.

"Tell her I'm sorry I was a dick that summer I was sixteen, when Dad left." Ariel finished his thought in my head.

"Ariel?" Doreen said. "Aw, honey."

He started to cry. The sound in my head was somehow worse than the feel of his blood going cool in between my fingers.

Taryn stared at his body, gritted her teeth, and motioned us forward.

As we moved, they talked amongst themselves in my head, trying to figure out what was going on. In training, they'd had us test up to five patches at a time. All AI is designed to feel like real people. Technically, a keeper could hold up to twenty patches, but five was the limit of testing. I had no idea how many they'd actually tested on a Keeper. Even in training, it had been intense. Five voices rattling amongst your own thoughts. Five different personalities all giving advice. But five people I actually knew. Five familiar voices were so much more. I wanted to tell them to be quiet and couldn't bring myself to—they'd be quiet for so long once I got them home, once their families talked to them one last time, and then nothing for eternity.

We had hit the clearing. We had to move fast and carefully. I listened for any drones, for any movement, but heard nothing. In my head, Blake yelled, "Now!" and I ran. Caleb and Taryn in front of me. It felt like miles, though it was only hundreds of feet, and then we were in the woods.

Once, shortly after we got married, Evan had explained the way we measure the brightness of planetary objects. The brighter they were, the lower their absolute magnitude. I'd liked the term. Absolute magnitude. When stars began to dim, it was called extinction. I wish I'd understood the concept enough to have explained it to Caleb as we patrolled at night, as he pointed out the stars. Everyone knew that sometimes the stars you see have been dead for years, but I thought it was beautiful. How long it took to dim to our eyes, how the light lasted so long it could reach us. In the woods, moonlight caused the moisture on leaves to glisten. It was somehow brighter than when we'd been in the city.

"Something's not right," Van said.

"I told you," Blake said.

I asked them what it was.

"Listen," Angie said.

I stilled my breath. Tried to listen past the sounds of Caleb and Tarun crunching their feet across the ground. There was something un-woods like. Electric.

"Stop," I whispered to Taryn and Caleb. They both stopped in their tracks.

Electric. Like the air after lightning.

I walked to the closest tree. I reached out and tapped the tree. The bark was bark, but it buzzed lightly. I ran my fingers until I found a break, and traced the break down until I found a panel. Traced fingers until I felt what must have been a very tiny lens.

"There's cameras out here," I said.

"What?" Taryn asked.

"Cameras in the trees."

"Shit, I knew it was creepy," Blake said. But the others hushed him.

I motioned Taryn and Caleb down until we were belly to the ground. I had no idea if it actually put us out of camera eyeline or not. But I hoped it gave them some sense of control. I wish I felt some.

In my head, they discussed my tactic and decided it was foolish. I wasn't going to argue.

We crawled forward through the woods. We only had to make it through the woods, and we'd come to the main road to Outpost 79. The main road would be dangerous, but fast-moving. If we could capitalize on the dark, we might make it.

In the dark, we heard another explosion from somewhere in the city we'd left behind.

"I was so scared of fireworks when I was a kid," Angie said. "Those booms waking me up. I always forgot what they were, I always thought we were under attack."

"And you joined…the military?" Doreen asked. The mom in her voice so strong.

"What else was I supposed to do?" Angie laughed but didn't explain.

As we reached the edge of the woods, Taryn grunted hard. As if she had withheld a scream. I crawled closer to her and saw what she had seen. A squad of bodies in front of us, sprawled in positions of pain. It looked like they'd been hit with a blast of some kind. Four or five people. The other squad at our Outpost.

It was only a couple of hours since we'd messaged them. Long enough for their patches to have remained active. I crawled between bodies, unclipping patches and adding them to my helmet. As each clicked into place, a voice that I recognized. Squads in a shared Outpost tended not to talk a ton, always on alternate patrols, but I knew them all by sight if not by name.

"We don't know what hit us, Keeper." Their CO, a tall man with a deep voice whom I'd shaken hands with once when I first arrived.

Their own Keeper happened to be the last patch I added.

"I messed up, I stayed back to get them all, and it's why I got hit."

I told him he didn't mess up, that was what he was supposed to do.

"No, save who you can," he said.

They began to talk with my own squad, all of them offering ideas of what was going on. So many voices. I was up to ten. They drowned out my own thoughts. Bickering possibilities.

The pain in my head had begun as a headache at my temples, a pulsing with my heartbeat. My eyes went in and out of focus. As we moved forward, I felt something wet on my face. My nose bled out of one nostril in a thin trickle. I wiped it away. Out of my corner vision, I saw a deer running. My body jolted, but then the deer was gone. There weren't any native to this area. In my head, they were all talking, talking. Their words blending together.

"Are you okay, Kendra?" At first, I thought it was in my head, but then Caleb reached out and touched my shoulder. It felt like he was reaching through something thick and flowing to touch me.

"Just need to keep going," I said.

Beside me, Evan was walking with me. He pointed to the sky, said, "Listen to the stars. They're getting so loud."

On my other side, Doreen was holding a bird. "Look, Kendra. It's moving."

The bird had the eyes of a child. It looked up at me, blinked.

"Kendra."

Taryn was in front of me. We'd paused movement. We couldn't stay still.

"I am giving you permission, Keeper, to remove your helmet," she said.

We'd been taught one thing in training: never remove a helmet that holds a patch. The connection would be disrupted, and the patch might fail, you might lose the person you were carrying. Even for a moment.

"I'm okay, I'm okay," I said.

The blood from my nostril reached my lips. The salt sharp and bitter.

"You can let us go," Doreen said. From inside my head, or standing beside me, or from another room.

"I'm okay," I repeated, and I adjusted the helmet, making sure it was snug. "We need to keep moving."

Taryn kept her eyes on me for a moment longer, and then we began our trek forward again.

The night sky was cloudy. The extra dark keeping us covered for now.

Next to me, a woman walked. She was juggling knives.

"Abby," Ariel said in my head.

A memory of a knife slipping. Her hand bleeding, and I was tenderly wrapping it in gauze. "Too many knives in the air," she said. And I laughed. Then she was laughing too.

The woman stopped walking, touched my shoulder. She held a finger to her lips. Her fingers were knives. An explosion lit up the night somewhere miles off.

Taryn motioned us forward, no time to calculate how far away the danger was.

When the drone came. It didn't make a sound that I could hear over their voices in my head. There was just Taryn pushing Caleb and me to the ground. We rolled to the side. No cover, and the drone was already speeding away. I didn't realize it'd shot until Caleb pointed at Taryn. Her eyes open, staring upwards.

Another patch. Click.

"Something isn't right," she said inside my head.

"No shit, ma'am," Blake.

"Kendra, you need to get off the main road. If you and Caleb go along the river, you'll have more cover."

"That's several miles longer," Blake said.

"More cover," Taryn said.

"Concur," Blake responded.

"I think they should remain on the road," said the other squad's CO. "Direct, fast."

They began to argue back and forth. I motioned Caleb off the road; we scuttled towards the river.

"I have seniority," the other CO said.

"Not in my fucking squad, you don't," Taryn replied.

We moved along the river, higher grass, more cover. Everything in me ached. My head pounded. Their voices scattered in and out, as if they were playing through a car radio going in and out of tunnels. Something was wrong.

In the river, sunlight sparkled on the water even though it was still night. A blue kayak went passed us. Caleb didn't pay any attention to it. The kayaker turned to face me, but had no face, just blank skin. They raised a hand and waved.

I heard the moaning before we saw the body. A man wearing the uniform of the place we were in. He was bleeding from multiple wounds. At first, I thought I wasn't seeing anything real but then Caleb said, "Shit."

I moved towards the man. His helmet was slightly askew, blood everywhere. He looked at me, eyes so scared. "Why did you?"

"Did what?" I asked.

"We aren't at war."

"You attacked us," Caleb said.

The man shook his head through the pain. The movements each sent a shuddering pain through his body.

"Leave him," someone said in my head.

His helmet. I saw the patches clicked into place. I didn't know they had Keepers. He saw what I noticed. "Can you carry them?"

I nodded.

"What are you doing?" Taryn asked.

I began to remove each patch from his helmet, clicking them into my own. He said, "I said I'd get them to 79."

"You will," I said.

Caleb watched me but didn't say anything or try to stop me.

In my head, they were arguing.

"She's a Keeper," I heard Blake's voice loudest, drowning out the others.

As the patches clicked in, I heard voices joining the chorus. They all began to argue again. Each yelling at the others about who did what.

The man in front of me said, "It's so quiet now. Oh, I hear it. I hear it."

But he was gone before he said what he heard. I added his patch.

Caleb looked back towards the river, "We have to keep moving. Daylight is catching up to us."

I had noticed it too, the warming of the sky.

The pain was taking over. Both nostrils bleeding now. The voices louder and louder. They had begun to get jumbled. I was losing some of them.

Ahead of me, a little girl ran. A deer jumped. Then the sky was falling, fireworks. Bright bursts of color.

Caleb took my hand, pulling me forward with him.

Fire. Works.

All their voices were getting panicked and loud.

They'd trained us that if we focused on a memory, we could stabilize them sometimes if we were getting overwhelmed.

A memory of being in the backseat of my parents' car. It was winter and night, and snow was falling. My parents' voices hushed to not wake me, but I was already awake. I peeked out between mostly closed eyes. Music on the radio.

Doreen had begun to hum along. Then Blake. Ariel. Angie. They were humming along to the radio. The voices getting softer. Soon, even the voices I didn't recognize. All humming in unison.

"Hey, what are you doing?" Caleb said.

A soldier in front of us.

"Kendra, shoot him," Blake whispered.

The soldier was raising a gun at Caleb, and it was as if everything was going so fast and slow. He didn't have a uniform. Nothing to reveal who he was with. Just the gun, and then my gun.

He had no patch. No sign of who he was.

Caleb looked for some identification. Nothing. A ghost.

On the ground, his blood spread like cracks in the ground after drought.

We kept moving forward through the receding darkness. Then Outpost 79.

This is my war story. So it ends when we enter the safe zone. The medics rushing to assess us. Someone asking us who we were, where we came from. Someone saying I was carrying too many patches. But I refused to let them be removed. The helicopters coming to take us home. Blood and sound. Fireworks. Music on the radio.

This is my war story. So it ends when we land on home soil, when the patches are removed one by one. When each family is given some remembrance. When they even take the other side's patches home. When they say we were attacked by unknown enemies. When the war starts. When Caleb calls me months later and asks what I think of what's happening, and I tell him I don't know anymore.

This is my war story. So it ends when I'm home and sleeping next to Evan, and I can finally sleep through a night.

This is my war story. So it ends when they say there will be no lingering effects, but sometimes I'll still hear one of their voices inside the voice of someone else, see them out of the corners of my eye.

This is my war story, so it ends when I finish telling it. I carried them home through the dark. I carried them so far. Listen, you can hear them.

A Sound Past Breaking

I pass a graveyard on the way back to my apartment every night. It doesn't bother me, not even after the dead start to show up at my door. I guess they sense something in me when I walk past them. Maybe it is a willingness to listen, or maybe it's something else, and I just don't want to name it.

Three knocks on the door mean that the visitor is a ghost. Ghosts won't hurt me, although they will definitely irritate me. Ghosts have a tendency to talk about their lives in "could haves" and "should haves" and "oh but I would haves." I always hold my tongue instead of blurting out that they didn't, and that is all that ended up counting for anything. It aches to not say what I mean, but I suppose it is better than just not meaning what I say.

The first ghost of the night is a girl that I used to know. She went to high school with me. She stares at me wistfully as if the years that I have gained on her are the most beautiful thing in the world. She talks about how she could have gone to a movie that night and how she should have been driving more carefully, and oh, how she would have loved college. I tell her that she didn't miss much. No, I don't. I never do. I just hold her hand and listen until she disappears. Then I return to my position on the floor, staring at a painting that hangs on my wall. The painting is of the child who was blessed by Death. She stands alone in a room surrounded by millions of flickering candles. I sigh because I always have to breathe a sigh of relief after the ghosts leave. It is only as the breath fills my chest that I think about the fact of breathing. I wonder if ghosts miss it, that pleasant release.

They first started coming to me on a Sunday. I am lying on my living room floor watching back-to-back episodes of *Battlestar Galactica.* The end of the world suddenly seems so preferable to being here. This is how most of my nights go. I keep expecting the phone to scream again and this time tell me that everything was a mistake. But then there is a knock at the door, and suddenly I have something to do.

It's a little girl at my door. I figure that it must be Halloween. It is October; I know that one true fact at least. The blood coming from her eyes looks so realistic. Then she reaches out and touches me. Her tiny hand on mine. The feeling is hard to describe. It is like a shiver that tickles the arch of my foot and kisses the back of my knees before flooding my stomach like a drink of ice water and stops the air in my lungs before I exhale it in a little cloud of breath. Honestly, it's not actually unpleasant, just sort of unexpected. The little girl smiles at me and absentmindedly brushes a bloody tear from her cheek. I have never been fond of children, but I feel compelled to invite her in. I go to my kitchen and bring her a brownie and a glass of milk. I'm not sure if ghosts can eat, but luckily, she can. She delicately picks up the square of gooey chocolate and shoves it into her mouth. I ask her how she can pick it up. I hope that I am not being rude or livingist. She tells me that ghosts can pick up most things. Then she asks me to tell her a story, the one that her mother used to tell her. She can't remember what the story was about, though. I tell her instead about the young girl who lived in a city where no one ever slept.

Every store in the city stayed open all night, but the owners never remembered to unlock their doors. The young girl really wanted to go into one of the stores and buy a dress that she saw in the window. The dress was made of the night sky, and it would change depending on the mood of its wearer. Sometimes it would become covered in clouds, sometimes the aurora borealis would shimmer across the fabric, and sometimes one might even notice a shooting star light a path from the neckline to the hem of the dress. The young girl wanted this dress so badly that she could barely breathe. So she boldly went up to the doors of the shop and knocked. Once. Twice. Thrice. Then even four times. But, of course, no one answered because the owners were carefully writing up their accounts of all the business that they hadn't done. So, the young girl did what no one had ever done, and she smashed her fist through the glass doors. As I say these words, I notice that the little ghost girl has finally closed her eyes. She begins to vanish: first her bare feet, then her body and her pink jumper, and then her face. It is probably for the best that she vanished because I'm not sure how I could finish the story. I had based it on a dream that someone once told me about, and really, I should have known better than to make a dream into a tale.

Pounding knocks mean that the visitor is a zombie. Zombies are always angry. They yell and make emphatic gestures with their rotting hands. I can't handle a zombie tonight. So I ignore the slamming of decaying fists. At least zombies give up easily, all the pounding makes them hungry, and they end up wandering off with no memory of why they came to see me.

Zombies are rarer visitors than the others. I don't know if this is because they are less common or if they just have less to talk about. They aren't as violent as the movies would make them out to be. Yes, they yell and scream. But they never do it at me. Their rage is directed at something else, something nameless. One, a young man who would have been inordinately handsome if half his face wasn't ripped away, didn't even say any words. He simply stared at me and howled. I wonder what the neighbors must have thought.

His howl reminded me of the sound that I almost made when I found out. I think that people expected me to scream, to show dramatic Oscar anguish. Maybe it scared them when I just simply stared into their eyes. I remember how they tried to tell me. They talked around the end result. There are certain words that can't be said out loud. I think they thought that a lack of details would make it easier for me. They said that it was because of a joke that he was telling. Although someone else contradicted this and said that he was silent. I prefer the version where he was about to laugh. It makes it seem less serious and more impossible. He used to raise his eyebrows the slightest bit when he was about to tell a joke. They told me that someone shoved him and that no one knew how hard his head hit the curb. They didn't know.

And then they would look away from me, and here is another thing that they couldn't know: that every night after that, I would be ripped from sleep by the sound of a skull cracking. So I moved to be closer to him. I don't tell people that because they would give me eyes like I was a poor thing, and I don't need that.

Two taps, very light but persistent, are the sign of a vampire. I only talk with them in the hallway. I'm smarter than to invite one in, because the next thing I know, it would probably be coming around for chips and gossip. Vampires are needy. They'll talk and talk until I want to slap some jumbo-sized crosses on my door.

Tonight's vampire is a new turn. He stares at my neck while we talk. But it's not a lustful, hungry look. It's more of a how-the-hell-can-I-manage-that look. Necks are beautiful, but they can also be intimidating. All that flesh that has to be gotten through to get at the sweet nectar. It's kind of like a pineapple. Sure, I can peel it and core it and slice it, or I could just pick up a can of pretty little rings. The vampire begins to talk about his ex-girlfriend from when he was alive. He says that she never understood him. Then he oh-so casually leans towards me, and I can see my own veins reflected in his eyes. He is trying to gauge the proper biting angle for future reference. I wonder if it's worse to be a short vampire or a really tall vampire. I really should start wearing more turtlenecks.

One vampire I met once told me that being bitten was the most amazing and revelatory experience that someone could have. He said that your life flashes before your eyes; or rather, not your life, but instead the life that you should have led, the life that you might have led if you had made just one small, insignificant choice in a different manner. I asked him what he saw, and he shrugged. I didn't push because everyone must have their secrets. Secrets are what give shape to our souls.

Some nights I wonder why I keep doing it. I keep answering the door and listening. I suppose the truth is ridiculously obvious. I keep hoping that the next knock will be the knock.

Three knocks. Pounding. Two taps. The next knock will be my invitation to dance off to the dirt.

I wait on the couch, eating a slice of Spanish Bun Cake and listening to the silence of no footsteps in the hall. Then there is a knock. One knock and then nothing. I run and throw open the door. There is just the hallway with the deep brown carpet and the walls that are painted sky blue. Across the way, one of my neighbors is putting her key into her lock. She is carrying a bag of groceries. She looks up and sees me. I want to ask her if she saw someone, but I don't. I just nod the neighborly nod that I've learned so well. She nods back and looks as if she is about to say something. But, she doesn't. She just goes into her apartment and shuts the door. I hear her lock turn, gently securing her from the world. And now there is just me and the empty hallway as it stretches out past all the welcoming doors.

I practice a card trick that someone once showed to me. When they did the trick, they could make it so that all the queens in the deck would disappear. I've been trying to learn it. I think the ghosts might enjoy it. But I can never get it quite right. Sometimes only one of the queens will disappear, or three of the kings, or two of the aces, and once even the entire deck of cards. There must be some turn of the hand that I'm missing. There must be some invisible piece that will make everything work. I always practice it before going to bed. I spread the cards out, shuffle them, and carefully deal them into piles. One. Two. Three. Four.

I go to bed early but don't actually close my eyes. I watch as a cast of shadows creep up my wall. I give them each names. It looks like some of them are having conversations. They are talking about shadowy things: the pain of soft lighting and the price of elongated clothing. Some of them seem to be praying, shadow hands clasped together or counting beads. Some of them are walking their shadow pets. Some of them could be dancing, and some of them could be falling.

I pass a graveyard on the way back to my house every night. It doesn't bother me, not even after the dead start showing up at my door. Sometimes I will pause at the graveyard gates for a second. I will reach out and caress the metal bars that separate the living from the dead. They always feel so icy, like when I would stand outside as a child and let snow dust my face. Except it's not really like that. It is a harder cold, the kind that twists inside my bones. I will stare out at the rows and rows of welcoming gravestones. All those names and numbers etched permanently into stone. All of those stories that never got whispered into children's ears and the lips that could no longer linger on their lover's skin. We don't become dust. We become the space between dates. And there is no sound there in that space, no voices, just the wind as it embraces the trees. So sometimes I will call out to the silence, "Please. Tonight. Please."

Someone Else's Sleeper

"I have such common dreams," a woman on the bus said into her phone. I tried not to look back at her, to stare too much. No one likes an eavesdropper. She had a nice voice, though, smooth—I imagined that on the radio, she would have no vocal fry. "Oh, you know, exams and mazes and shit."

The bus stopped just as I was about to sneak a look. It was my stop, and so I controlled the urge and got off. As the bus pulled away, I felt the shakes in my hands. I clenched my hands into fists, fingernails digging into the skin of my palms where the indents had left bruises that had begun to seem permanent, and walked the block home.

The apartment was dark, Forest wasn't home, and I wondered if he would be. Some weeks I barely saw him, we lived such opposite lives. Our conversations, when we did see each other, circled around his boyfriend, his classes, his job as a research assistant. He never asked how I was doing, never noticed the darkness that hung beneath my eyes. I was alright with that.

I looked in the fridge and pulled out a tub of miso. Heating up some water, I thought back to the woman. A shudder ran through my skin. I leaned back against the counter, bracing myself against the feeling.

On the stove, the water began to boil. I watched the bubbles of water popping on the surface until the shudder had passed.

My sister called me that night. I sat on my bed, with the lights off, as she talked. If I couldn't see anything of my room, I could imagine I was home and she was talking to me from across the bedroom we'd shared all through our childhood. I could imagine she was telling me secrets about the boys she had a crush on and the teachers she hated.

"Harvey has been working doubles," she said. "We barely ever are in bed at the same time. Sometimes I have to go in and curl up by the girls, just so I can get some sleep, you know?"

"Will that last long?" I asked. I reached my free hand out, clenching and unclenching my fist.

"He's trying to get it switched. He knows I can't sleep alone," she said. "I'm not like you, Es." I heard the tone in her voice: was it jealousy, or was it knowing?

"How are the girls?" I asked.

She sighed. "They're good. They take after Harvey so much. It's strange sometimes to think they belong to me, too."

I pictured them in my head: the twins, always in contrasting shades of identical outfits.

"But you know, I wish sometimes they were more like us," she said.

"You do?" I asked. She didn't respond right away, but I heard her breathing, knew she hadn't hung up. "Why?"

A longer pause still. "We're strong, Es. We're so strong."

"Miss?" A man's voice. I turned, and he was leaning over the counter. Thirties, too snug t-shirt and jeans—showing off the curves of his muscles as if he'd put on clothes the right size and they'd shrunk during the day. "Can you help me find this book?"

I stood up, forced a smile onto my face. "What book?"

"I wrote the call number down, but I can't find it on the shelf." He held up a tattered slip of paper.

"Of course," I said. I stepped outside of the service area and followed the man deep into the stacks. He walked slightly ahead of me. The book's call number was in one of the farthest back areas of the library. He stepped into the row and I followed.

"I can't find it anywhere."

"Did you look at the shelf above and the shelf below? That's normally where they get misplaced. People always think they can remember the shelf, don't look at the numbers, and put the book back on the wrong one," I explained.

"No, I didn't. Stupid of me," he said. I heard a tone in his voice, a slight edge of amusement that I didn't like. I could feel the spiders on my skin. He handed me the slip of paper, and I bent down to retrieve the text. As I did, he pressed himself against me.

I stood up quickly, spinning around and pushing him back into the shelf behind him. The look of amusement in his eyes switched quick to anger.

"Hey—" he began.

I shook my head, grabbing hold of his arm. I let my nails dig into his palm. "Do you take things from people?" I asked.

"What the fuck do you mean?" he asked. His voice came out ragged, a whisper, when I knew that he wanted to shout. I let the fear play across him. "I don't take shit."

"Well, I do," I said.

That night I dreamed of a bar, a woman dancing on the counter. I dreamed of heat and limbs and the press of her body against a wall. As she moaned, we fell backwards through the concrete and into a forest. Except the trees were only sculptures of trees. I looked up as leaves began to fall off of them. Paper leaves, dripping with green ink still fresh on them.

In the morning, I ate a bowl of cereal as I leaned against the counter. Forest stumbled out of his bedroom and almost jumped when he saw me. "Jesus, Es. I didn't hear you get up."

"I didn't even know you were home," I replied.

He nodded, taking a bottle of water from the fridge. "I got home late."

"Explains it. I slept so deep last night," I said. I tipped the cereal bowl to my face and let the cold milk pour into my mouth. It tasted so sweet and icy and creamy. It was the best thing I'd eaten in weeks because everything was heightened, fresh.

"You must have. You look really good," Forest said. He sipped his water, studying me. "If I didn't know any better, I'd say you had a really good fuck."

"Better," I said. "Dreams."

I walked to the coffee shop that I liked best for a treat. I wanted a raspberry latte when I could taste it. My favorite barista, Conor, was at the counter. He'd been working there as long as I'd been going, two years or so. I liked his voice, the way he moved when he made coffee, his laugh. He smiled when he saw me, and I felt my heart beat a step quicker.

"Es! I thought you must have found a better coffee place."

"Nope, just off coffee for a bit," I said.

"We don't encourage that. Caffeine's the one addiction I highly advise people to stick with. You don't want to be a quitter, right?" He studied me as he spoke. Perhaps he was trying to pinpoint whatever was different about me. He wouldn't guess it.

"I'm definitely not a quitter. Make me the largest raspberry latte you've got," I smiled, and it felt natural for the first time in weeks.

"On it." He spun around towards the espresso machine. All of his movements were practiced and easy. I wondered if he recreated the motions in his sleep, even. He had lovely hands, I could see the muscles and tendons moving under his skin as he twisted knobs, pulled levers.

And he made the latte too quickly, spinning back to me before I could avert my eyes and hide the fact that I'd been watching him. He held my gaze as he placed the cup into my hands. Our fingers brushed. It sent a shiver up my skin, but one that felt like dipping into a cold pool on a hot day.

"I wanted to ask you for your number," he said. I liked the directness of it. He didn't build into it, didn't try flirting. "I'd been wanting to and then you disappeared for a while. But I even had a dream about it."

I didn't even flinch at the word; I was so full. "A dream about asking for my number?"

"I like dreams when other people are in them. Sometimes I like to dream things so I know how to do them when I wake up," he said.

134

It sounded strange, but strange in the way that other people's dreams often did.

I wrote it down for him. As I left, I took a sip of the latte and the raspberry tasted sweet and tart and warm under the coffee.

My phone buzzed in my pocket before I was even halfway home. He asked if I wanted drinks later, and so I responded yes before I could remember to say no.

"You have a date? Like a date with a person?" Forest practically shouted his questions, as if I was hard of hearing instead of hard of relationships.

"The barista, Conor, from the coffee shop. And it's just drinks," I said.

"Oh, him," Forest said. "The one who you're always comparing to a dancer in your head?"

I glared at him. "I never told you that."

"I've watched you watch him. I practically can see you reciting ballet terms." He chuckled for a second. "Remember in undergrad when you dated that guitarist?"

"Yes, why?" I played impatience.

"You dreamed of guitar riffs for weeks. Will you dream about coffee now? Just steamy, steamy milk?" He laughed, delighted with himself.

And now I didn't need to play. "I won't be doing that."

Forest saw the change in my face and shrugged. "You used to be more fun."

"I used to be a monster," I said. I left the room.

I dressed simple. Tights, dress that was short in the right places, but not too short. He'd chosen a bar not far from where I lived, so I walked. I never felt worried walking at night. People usually knew not to step too close.

The bar was small, fairly well lit, blues on the stereo. It felt more inviting than I'd expected. Conor was already there, at a small table tucked in the corner. He stood up when I entered. I walked over to him.

He pulled out my chair, which felt too quaint. "I don't know why I did that. I've never done that."

I laughed. "Thanks, though." I took my seat, and he sat back down across from me.

Someone came over and took our order.

"So, is it weird to see me outside the café?" he asked.

"Well, I mean, no. I kind of realized that you didn't live there," I said.

"Fair point. It's just I've never asked a customer out, and it feels strange," he said.

"In a bad way?" I asked. I wondered if he was seeing what he should have seen in me—the emptiness hungering its way through my body.

"No, no, definitely not," he said quick.

And then the conversation eased. It was like he had tested the ice on a lake, found it was solid, and then the walk across became easy. He was a grad student, which I'd never known, studying Modernist literature. He was delighted to find out I worked in a library. "Why have we never talked about books?" he asked. And then we did. We talked about which book made us love them when we were young, the authors who we cyber-stalked to find out when they'd have new books coming out so we could order them months in advance, the physical aspect of books that we liked best—he was for the smell and I was for the feel, the weight of certain books in my hands.

I wanted him, wanted to take him home and fall into him so easily.

"Hey," someone said and snapped us out of the shelter of words we'd been building around ourselves. I turned, and my body jolted. It was tight clothes from the library. He was paler, drawn around his eyes. After only one time. What weakness, I thought and then I pushed the thought away. It was something the old me would have thought.

"Do I know you?" Conor asked him.

But he wasn't looking at Conor. He stared at me. "You're from the library right?"

I nodded. He didn't remember me. How deep had I dug into him? How greedily had devoured?

"I thought so. You're real familiar. Were you there yesterday? I fainted or something, and I couldn't sleep all night. It was like I had nothing in my head, and that sounds like a good thing, right, but, like, it was more like I wanted to have something in my head, but I just couldn't find it." His voice rattled out.

Conor studied him. Maybe trying to figure out what the guy was on.

"Oh?" I said. "You should see a doctor."

The guy stared hard at me. "Can books like infect you? Like mold?"

I shrugged. "You really should see a doctor."

The guy nodded. He turned and began to walk away. I felt my body ease. Conor smiled at me, he was thinking about something. "Weird, huh?"

"Yeah, weird," he said.

And we returned to talking.

It was nearly midnight when we walked to my apartment. Then inside to my bedroom. Then onto my bed. We were kissing and his mouth tasted warm. His hands were on my thighs, under the skirt of my dress. I pushed up his shirt, felt his chest, his heart beating under the skin, under the muscles and bone. He pulled down my tights quickly. His hands moving with as much precision as when I watched him making coffees. I undid his jeans, ran my hands up and down him. For a second, I thought about pushing him away, about not making this mistake. But I wanted him so much, and so I just kissed him harder.

After he lay next to me and I felt the sweat cooling on my skin. I shivered with it. "You can't sleep here," I said.

He took a second to respond. I heard a catch in his breath before he did. "You don't want me to stay."

"No, I do. But. If you sleep here, you'll regret it," I said.

He turned onto his side, watched me. "What do you mean?"

"I won't mean to do it. But I'll take your dreams. I'll do it while you sleep, pull them from your body. I can't help myself." I couldn't look at him.

He laughed for a minute, saw that I wasn't breaking, wasn't smiling to show him that it was a joke. "You're not kidding? You think you'll take my dreams?"

I turned to face him. "I don't have my own. So I take them. And I don't want to take them from you."

"Explain," he said. "Please."

So I did. It started when I hit puberty. My sister had done the same thing before me. I'd had insomnia for weeks. Then I was at a sleepover and I'd had the best sleep of my life. All the other girls' dreams feeding me all night long. It had felt so good and I'd been so greedy, I'd pulled their dreams without knowing what I was doing, so hungrily that one of the girls never dreamt again. She withered away. Every day at school, she'd look more and more like a husk. Until she just didn't show up for school anymore. I'd done that. My parents assured me that I hadn't known what I was doing and I hadn't. But that didn't mean I didn't blame myself. I learned to go without dreams for months at a time, sleeping the bare minimum for survival. Such emptiness always awaiting me when I closed my eyes. It was so cold and so dark without anything to fill the sleep. In college, I'd date off and on, just a dream here and there. Enough to sustain. And then I fucked up. The guitarist. I let him sleep over too many times. I dreamed his dreams. They were filled with so much sound and I couldn't get enough of them. It was only when he stopped playing music, started staring too long off into the distance as if he saw something there that he didn't quite recognize, that I realized that I had gone too far.

So I stopped altogether. One dream every three months. I'd take them from Forest because he knew I needed them, because he agreed. It wasn't easy. A state of constant exhaustion, heaviness. I fought the sleep with pain, fingernails into skin.

And, of course, the occasional accident. Only they weren't accidents. The man at the library, the stranger in an elevator once who called me a bitch under his breath because I didn't want to talk to him, the woman who walked her dog by yanking his leash so harshly. I'd dig my hands in and take the dreams right out of them, even when they were awake, even when they were staring at me in such terror.

"What if I say I don't believe you? That I want you to prove it to me?" Conor said.

"You'll regret it," I said.

"Try me." He touched the side of my face, ran a finger down the curve of my face. "I've always been good at dreaming."

In my dream that night, I was walking through a city I'd never been in. Everyone was dressed for summer: women in sundresses and little girls in bright pinks and purples. A man was selling ice cones at the far end of the street. He handed one to me, drenched in bright blue syrup and I sucked it as I walked toward the far end of the street which opened into the ocean. I kept walking until the water was lapping at my feet. The sun felt so warm.

"Es," Conor said from behind me. I turned to him and he was wearing a shirt that was the exact same shade of blue as the sky.

"You're in your own dream," I said.

"It's our dream," he said. He took my hand and I felt electricity, felt cold water on a hot day. We walked into the ocean, until it was up to our waists. He put his arms around me.

"Do you trust me?" he asked.

And I did.

He dunked us under the water. Everything above shimmered and shook with the waves.

And then we both woke up.

In the Dark, They Say You Can't See What's Coming For You

In the middle of the pandemic, the highways were always empty. It was funny, I'd once said to Mark, that when the world is falling apart, is the one time ambulances make good time.

The first we'd been to was already too late. A woman with her throat ripped out by her toddler. The child escaped somewhere. I don't know if they were ever found, though I've always hoped that they were, that someone kept them locked up long enough for the doctors to do their thing and figure out how to bring people back. It didn't take as long as anyone thought it would. But it took probably longer than an infected toddler had.

I wondered sometimes, still, if Mark had worried about the infected. If he had imagined their lives after they were cured. I wondered sometimes, still, if Mark had thought about it after the bite and before the turn. If he'd imagined all of the infected we'd seen race into the dark, escape through windows. Or if he'd thought of the bodies, all the bodies, we'd called on scene. All I could know for sure was that he'd raised his hand up to me, that he'd shown me the bite above his wrist instead of hiding it, pulling his sleeve down to cover it. He'd shown me so I could back my way to the ambulance, climb inside, lock the doors. We hadn't known then what I knew now.

One of our first rides together, we'd been called to a lake where a little girl had fallen through the ice. Her skin had the lightest edge of blue, where she was laid on top of the white snow. People were gathered around, one man giving CPR desperately. Mark had been so gentle, one hand gently hovering on the man's shoulder. He'd checked vitals, even though he knew, we both knew, that she was long past gone. The coroner's team was already there, right behind us. As they began to zip the body bag closed, Mark had brushed a strand of hair from the girl's face, away from the zipper, so it wouldn't catch. If I'd been the one to give his eulogy, write his obituary, I'd have said that.

It was a routine call. Or routine for the pandemic. Someone saying they'd been hurt, and us assuming that meant bit, but they didn't want to say. That they were hoping they'd be the miracle who just needed a stitch.

When we got there, we let out a sigh of relief, because it was a woman sitting on the curb. She had a clear sprained ankle, swollen. But otherwise, she looked fine, no sign of bites or infection. She said she'd tripped. Mark was wrapping her ankle when a group of infected emerged from behind the house, probably drawn by the woman's yelps of pain or the sound of our siren. One rushed me, tossed me to the ground as it leapt on top of me. A woman wearing a t-shirt that showed a fat cat and read, "I'm always hungry," and I almost laughed. Mark knocked her off me. The woman with the sprained ankle had already taken off running, fear overriding pain. "Run," Mark yelled, and I ran.

The police van that should've arrived at the scene before we did rounded the corner. Sirens wailing. That was protocol, police first, but we were always early. The infected turned from Mark to the sound, and he could've run to the ambulance, run to safety. But he raised his arm, showing the bite.

They made the announcement that night, that the infection could be cured. Mark must've been one of the last ones killed instead of tranqed. Imagine that, if he'd known that there was a cure, and he was just a couple of hours too soon, would he have thought it was funny? Funny in the way that the universe is.

The thing was, I'd already been scratched. I could feel it starting to burn. Scratches took longer than a bite, sure, but it still happened. As I watched him from the window, as I saw them shoot him down, it was too late. But a few moments earlier, I could have opened the door and welcomed him inside. We could've sat there in the ambulance, waiting for the news together. Maybe, in that version of events, it never would've come. Maybe, we would have sat there until the night enveloped us into whatever it was we became.

Stone Fruit

On Tuesdays, in town, the dead would occasionally come back for a slice of pie at the local train depot diner. The dead, Shelly noticed, were partial to the cherry pie. But, then again, who wasn't? It had an all butter crust, so flaky that crumbs would get everywhere no matter how dainty a nibbler you were. The filling was made from real Door County cherries, which the diner owners froze in huge batches every summer. Shelly liked making the filling, dumping the cherries into the mixing bowl, where the frozen orbs would ping against the metal. The red stained everything and she'd lost many a blouse sleeve to a splash. The key was a little bit of lemon juice, a little bit of orange peel, and the tiniest hint of clove—never pre-ground, you had to do it as you made the pie—and a little mahleb. You put the stone of the cherry alongside the fruit, the owners said, because then the pie knows it is whole. No one knew about the clove or mahleb, except the owners and Shelly. People would ask what the secret ingredient was and Shelly would whisper, "Just between you and me…. it's the moon."

The owners had let her in on the secret, a small gift from them, a "please the universe isn't all bad", after her sister had disappeared. It was what they could offer and Shelly kept it close to her. Shelly was 22 that year and her sister, Magdalene, was 15. Magdalene liked movies about real-life events, trying on shoes at the mall, and wanted to be an engineer. She also hated everything sometimes, would slam her door when irritated, and rolled her eyes at Shelly so hard that Shelly thought they might one day spin right out of her head. But those things were seldom, and human, and mostly Shelly loved Magdalene more than she loved the world.

Magdalene had been missing for five years and eleven days, but had never shown up on a Tuesday. Every time the diner bell dinged as the door swung open, Shelly would look up and there would be her old kindergarten teacher, Mrs. Rachelle, waving at her. Or the mayor from a hundred years before Shelly was born. Shelly wasn't a fan of his. He talked fast and with such bombast that Shelly could almost see exclamation points appear from his mouth like he was in a comic book. Or it would be someone else. Some dead who had decided to have a slice of pie on their day off from the afterlife. Shelly had worked every Tuesday for the past five years and eleven days, once even taking her shift when she had sprained her ankle so badly that she had to use crutches. The owners had helped her carry orders out to the tables. They watched her with the keen eyes of people who knew what it was like to have you heart jump into your throat at the sound of every doorbell.

On the fifth year and eleventh day, the Tuesday rush was slow. Only the living entered. Shelly took orders: less pie, more coffee, and meals. The living needed sustenance while the dead only needed taste. A regular flagged Shelly down for a refill. Mrs. Hamberlin came in almost every Tuesday on the off chance her husband would be able to come, and who when he did, would jump up and hug him. They'd hold each other so tightly for a moment, as if trying to crush the other, because they both knew how easy it was to never be able to hug the person you loved again.

"Did you hear, hon?" Mrs. Hamberlin asked Shelly, as she poured a mug back into coffee-filled.

"Hear?"

"The dead won't be coming back. The door is closed. Some bureaucracy." Mrs. Hamberlin fluttered one hand above her head, showing the silliness of the government.

Shelly swallowed hard. "I'm so sorry, Mrs. Hamberlin. Your husband—"

Mrs. Hamberlin shook her head. "I'm closer to him than here, anyway. But how are you?"

The woman studied her with kindness, and Shelly felt like she might float up and away. It was always when people were kind that she could feel everything. "I'll be fine. She never comes."

"Maybe that's because she's not there. Only the dead show up."

Shelly had never thought about it. Had never imagined a life for Magdalene. A runaway somewhere in a city unlike the town they grew up in. Maybe Magdalene was taking classes at the local tech college. Maybe she called herself something else: April or Ruby or maybe just Mary, because only she would get the joke. Maybe every Tuesday, she woke up, sipped tea, and didn't think about her sister at all.

Shelly let out an oof of breath. "Maybe."

That night, she cleaned up the diner. Pushed chairs in and refilled the ketchup bottles. The owners pointed to the cherry pie, unordered by anyone and still whole, and told her to slice some up for the three of them. She placed plates on the counter and cut too-large slices, so that they spilled over the edge of the wedge-shaped spatula she used to scoop them out. They sat around their slices in silence until Shelly took the first bite. The sour-sweet hit her tongue and the edge of bitter, of something unplaceable, yet exactly where it belonged.

"How did you decide on the recipe? The mahleb?" She asked, having learned the secret without ever hearing the path.

One of the owners smiled. "Our son, he used to say, 'Every sweet needs its sharp.' We found our sharp in mahleb."

Shelly licked the filling from her fork. She wondered how the dead slept that night, knowing they were far away from everything they'd once known. She wondered if her sister looked out the window, in some other place, and saw the moon.

Under the Surface, Under the Light

When they were training us, on the first day as they were double-checking that we could read the little meter that measured the amount of air we still had in our tanks, one of the teachers looked us up and down and said, "Never underestimate the water. It doesn't care about how much time you have left."

I'm not sure that any of us were really paying attention, not to him, when we were so focused on what the other teachers were saying. But it stuck in my head, swirling around like the memory of an accident that only almost happened, just waiting in your mind to wake you up in a panic sweat some night.

75 Minutes

The pool is 80 feet deep and 200 feet long, and 100 feet wide. The water it takes to fill it would run a town dry; so it never gets refilled, just cleaned—an endless cycle of pumps and filters. The first time I saw it, it was darker blue than any swimming pool I'd ever seen. I wanted to ask someone if that was because they used more chlorine or if it was just because of the size—but I never asked. It looked like the swimming pools I used to have in my dreams as a kid: the color was a little off, the depth a little unsure, so that the dreams could so easily slip between the fantastic and nightmares.

At the bottom of the pool, under all that water, was a replica of a station and pod. They were exact in dimensions and specs. Training in a neutral buoyancy pool would help us to train for EVAs before we reached space, or that was the idea—but, of course, everything could be controlled in the pool, and so, really, it wasn't like space would be at all.

There were twelve of us training that cycle. A slightly smaller group than usual. By the end of training, there would be nine—the smallest group to ever graduate the course.

I was having not particularly good, but still sort of satisfying, sex with one of the other trainees. Tenley had blond hair that she kept at a length between short and long, which irritated me on some level. She'd wear it pulled back, and an hour into the day, bits of her hair would have come loose from their holding and dangle around her face. When I had her against a wall, sometimes my gaze would fall to the freed strand of her hair as it bobbed in front of me, wiggling like a caterpillar caught on the thread of a spider web.

"Roll!" Tenley would shout before she took her dive, every time. She'd suit up, yell it, then place her helmet on.

It was Tenley's hair I'd think I was seeing when it happened—floating in front of me in the darkening of the pool. As the lights above flickered in and out and the blue got deeper and deeper.

70 Minutes

"Okay, but what about the idea that reality is really just this infinite loop?" Hana asked. She circled her hands around each other in the air as she said it.

"What does that even mean?" Alec had his feet up, leaning back. He made it look as if being in space was the most blasé thing in the world. I'd never seen his body in perfect, sitting up posture.

"Like I had this philosophy professor in college who said that there were a few people who posited the idea that life isn't necessarily a simulation, but that we can never really know if we're dead, because maybe we're all just living an imagined life in the moments before our death. Like we can't actually ever know when our lives stop, only other people can know that about us. So how can we ever know if what we're experiencing is real or is just a dream?" Hana got worked up about these kind of things. She'd start rambling, and most of us stopped listening. Or I did, at least, but her ramblings about death always pissed me off just a little bit more than the others.

"That's fucking ridiculous, Han. Death is concrete. People know when they're dying," I said.

She looked over at me, for a second shocked, and then she let it slip from her face. "Sorry, Riley."

I shrugged. "No sorries needed." But, after a few minutes, filled with the kind of awkward silence where everyone's breathing got accentuated until the air was thick with the hiss-puff of it, I got up and went to my bunk.

In bed was always the time I most realized I was in space. There was something about the way it felt—some deep in-the-bone tremble that I didn't notice in any other position. I tried describing it to Gage one time, a couple of years after he'd left the training and never looked up at the sky with the same wonder again, and he'd paused for a few moments. Then he said, "I felt like that at the bottom of the pool sometimes, like all that weightlessness made me feel extra heavy under my skin somehow." That hadn't been exactly what I meant, but I hadn't ever wanted to tell Gage that. I knew that he felt the water pressing in on him, even when he was far inland.

"Don't pay attention to Hana's theories. She's the reason we shouldn't let philosophy bros into space." Alec walked in and dropped himself onto his bunk.

Before I could answer, a humming sound filled the air—a slow peal that at first I thought was in my head until I saw the look of confusion on Alec's face. "Is that the fucking distress beacon?"

We both got up quickly and went to the control room. Hana and our captain, Vivian, were already there. Gael, the medic, rushed in a moment behind us. The beacon went silent.

"Was that an error?" Gael asked.

"I don't know. I'm trying to get confirmation. It was from the station we're headed to." Vivian pointed the location out on one of the screens: Lumiere Station. One of the leading research stations and the place we were supposed to be picking up a scientist and her research from. Vivian flipped on the mic in front of her, "Lumiere Station, this is BNNI-111, do you copy?"

Silence.

Vivian reached to touch the mic again, but before she could, a voice flickered out of the speakers, "Tank. We're going into the tank. Help. In the tank."

We waited for more, holding our breath in synchronized stillness, but the speakers said nothing.

60

You learn the water's surface before you learn its depth. We had to swim the length of the pool, back and forth, back and forth. My arms would ache so much at the end of the day that sometimes I couldn't lift them high enough to get food into my mouth. Gage was the one who thought of preparing protein smoothies beforehand so that we all could slump into chairs, slurping up the grainy drink through straws until we had de-nauseated ourselves enough to sleep.

I had dreams those nights about the pool, about the water underneath me, darkening until I was swimming above a night sky without stars. It was one of those nights when Tenley slipped into the bed with me, said, "You were whimpering. Bad dream?"

"Yeah, I guess."

"About the water?" she asked, and I turned to look at her. The room was dark, but a sliver of light came through the window and illuminated part of her face. She studied me with a look of understanding, and so I pulled her closer, kissed her, slipped my hand inside her panties. For a little while, I didn't think about the pool.

It was weeks of training before we got to do a simulated disaster. It was in a simulation when things went wrong.

We had to dock manually at Lumiere. A process that took longer than we would have liked, knowing that inside the station, people might be hurt. Hana and I were the most trained at EVA, so we were the ones who went out to release the docking bay door. As we were inputting the emergency code that opened it, Hana said, "Did you feel anything before it happened?"

"Before what?"

"Before the NBL accident? Did you have any omens? Know it was coming?" She whispered the questions, fast and quiet.

"Not a fucking clue," I answered, but I pictured a flash of hair, a light, and something swimming beneath the water---a long dark shape where no shape should have been. "Why?"

She was silent, watching as the bay door began to open. "My hands feel weird. The only time I ever remember them feeling like this was right before something really bad happened."

The door was almost completely open. "What happened?"

"Never mind," she said.

We watched as the ship entered the docking bay. We headed inside behind it.

"We are getting no responses, and we don't know what kind of situation will greet us. I've messaged our station and followed all standard procedures. I want to make sure that all of you understand that if you want, or need to, you may ask to remain with the ship. No one will judge you." Vivian said. She looked each of us in the eyes as she did so.

None of us said anything.

Inside the station, the first hallway was empty but unexceptional. Lights were on, nothing was damaged. It could have been a normal day between shifts. The first room we came to was a sleeping area. The beds were made. The room empty and neat. I saw a photo of a smiling little girl pinned to a wall. She looked seven or eight, a lifetime stretching ahead of her. I'd tracked down photos and vids of my training team, afterwards, as children. I'd stared into each face, still or flickering in image, and I'd try to place the childhood face with the adult ones I had grown to know. Tenley, as a child, smiled at the person taking the video. Gage was on a swing, laughing. Devon and Sidonie had known each other as children, their arms wrapped around each other's shoulders as they grinned into a camera lens. The others all began to blend together, each face promising some idea of what they would do with their lives. A history teacher once asked me if I thought we would still have wars if soldiers were required to look at the childhood photos of everyone they would have to fight against. I hadn't answered and the teacher had said, of course we would, it's easy to ignore things when we think we are right. At the time, I'd agreed with him. Later, I wasn't so sure.

We kept walking. The next room was the same, a little less neat, with an unmade bed. At the end of the hall, it branched in two directions. Hana and I took the left route while Gael, Vivian, and Alec took the right. We moved in silence. The first door we came to was a research station. There were aquariums set up on several tables. Inside, fish swam. I walked up to the closest tank and glanced inside. There were several fish inside, and some kind of kelp growing up from the bottom. "What do you think they were studying with fish?"

"It was something to do with the effects of algae and sea kelps creating oxygen in different water conditions? I can't quite remember, but I looked up Lumiere's research when I heard we were headed here," Hana replied. Of course, she had done her research. I'd just thought, *cool,* and hopped aboard. Hana walked to one of the far tanks; its water was darker than the others. Almost murky. She leaned forward to look inside. I turned away, but spun back when she let out a yelp.

"Jesus, what?"

She had stepped back from the tank, but stared at it. "There was something in the water."

"There's something in all of these tanks, Han." I gestured around the room.

"No, like. Something that didn't look right." She pointed.

I walked up to the tank and looked inside. In the murkiness, I could tell something was swimming. My stomach clenched for a moment—dark body in the water—but I pushed the thought away. I leaned closer, and it swam nearer. At first, it looked like just an eel, nothing strange about it, until it got closer and I saw its eyes. They were large and seemed to be lit up from within, emitting a faint glow. It blinked once. When its eyes reopened, the glow was gone.

"They glowed, right? You saw that too?" I asked Hana.

"Yeah, but there's something else too. They seemed…human?"

I looked back, and it was still looking out at me. It tilted its head upwards as if looking for my own eyes. I turned away. "Let's try looking in another room."

45

"This will be your longest dive. In it, you will be working to fix a leak somewhere aboard the station. However, you will first need to locate it. We have programmed three areas on the replica to emit a slight pulsing light, which you will need to find. These areas, once located, will need to be repaired. Your whole team will need to work in tandem, as all the areas must be repaired within the same time or the pulse will not turn off." The trainer spoke in a monotone, his voice so clipped and emotionless that I kept having to tap my leg to stay awake.

"This seems like the weirdest fucking sim. When would they ever have 3 malfunctions that had to be solved in tandem?" Gage asked from beside me.

"If there was an electric short, maybe?" Tenley said. It was an answer that didn't really make sense, but I nodded because an hour before we'd had sex in her bunk, and I was hoping to do it again after the sim.

Gage rolled his eyes. "Yeah, okay."

Devon and Sidonie were the first pair in the water. They'd even been on a swim team together in high school, and all of their movements in the water had the ease of years behind them. I admired their dive and watched as they slipped into the deeper blue.

Gage and I were the last pair. Tenley, Roll!, had already gone under. I looked up at the ceiling of the lab, forty feet above us, and it looked further away than it ever had. And then I was under.

Going down always seemed so fast, while the ascension would be painstakingly slow. The light at the bottom was minimal, our sightlines were maybe ten feet to twelve feet in any direction. Gage and I were checking the East end of the replica, we slowly moved along it—both looking at it and gently feeling it with our hands as we moved. It helped to keep a sense of orientation in the water. It was easy to become disoriented and lose your sense of where you were located physically in space. We had been down for maybe fifteen minutes tops, when our coms buzzed in our ears.

"Gage and Riley, we need you to move more quickly. We think Sid and Dev may be having some kind of issue. We lost their vid feeds. They should be maybe 5 minutes away from where you are, if you keep going forward."

Under the water, Gage shrugged his shoulder slightly. Under the water and the weight of his air tank, it was barely a movement at all, but I knew his expressions. We both were assuming this, too, was part of the sim. We picked up our pace, to the best of our ability, and moved forward.

I noticed the color change first. The dark bloom against the blue. At first, I thought my eyes were playing tricks on me. I blinked twice, hard. But the bloom remained. I followed it from a trail to a thicker portion, and then I saw the body. It was Devon, floating in the thickest part of the bloom. I realized it was his blood. His arms spread, gently billowing near him, made it seem like he could be fine.

156

The cracked open glass of his mask told me otherwise, though. He'd have drowned so quickly down there, no chance of getting to the surface in time. Gage still moved towards him, reached out, and grabbed Devon's arm. Then he let go. I glanced around for Sidonie or some sign of what had happened, and from the shadows of darkness around us, I thought I saw a shape in the water—something long and dark, like a shark but not quite a shark's shape. Sinuous was the word that popped into my head to describe its movement. I moved towards Gage, trying to get his attention, point it out, but he was already moving forward, looking for Sidonie. I turned back, and the shape had gone back beyond my sight line.

I knew I was imagining it, that we weren't really in the ocean or outer space, that it was a pool and there could be no living non-human thing down there. I knew it, and still I searched the shadows for signs of it coming back.

35

"I think we found something," Vivian's voice echoed out of our radio as we walked.

"Where are you?" Hana asked.

"We're at the main research bay."

We were not too far away, so we quickened our pace towards it. Vivian, Gael, and Alec stood at the main door. It was open, but they hadn't stepped inside. Hana and I both peered inside. I half-expected some scene of carnage, of massacre. Inside, though, was a giant covered pool. "What is it?"

"Why didn't I think of that?" Hana asked. "When they said tank, but I didn't think of it. I knew they had an isolation tank on the station. They were doing research on isolation as a way to calm people after emergencies or in stress situations."

We all stepped into the room together. Vivian walked up to the tank and pressed a hand against it, as if she'd feel something that would offer a clue. "Do you think everyone's inside there?"

Alec let out a snort of laughter and then caught himself, shaking his head. "This station had to have had at least twenty people on it. You think they're all in there?"

"Why would they be in there?" Gael asked.

None of us had an answer.

30

It was because of Sidonie that we let go of the replica. We saw her floating maybe eight feet away. Gage lifted his hand off, and then I followed suit. Both of us moved towards her, towards the shadowing darkness of the pool. As we got closer, she began to turn towards us, a slow spin that seemed graceful, like one of those dancers on a music box who turns with the song. Behind her in the darkness, a shape began coming closer. I saw the way the water moved around it. In front of my vision, a strand of blond hair floated. Where the fuck is Tenley? I thought.

The shape began to speed up, as Sidonie turned so slowly, the darkness got closer and closer. I saw the glint of eyes, a mouth preparing to open. Sidonie's eyes met mine as she completed her turn.

25

There were an entrance and an exit hatch on the top of the tank's cover. Both could be reached by ladders up the side of the tank. Vivian had climbed up and lifted the hatch. She called into the tank, "Hello?"

There was no answer. She turned on her flash beam and aimed it inside. "I can't see a fucking thing. Why are there just two hatches? Who designed this?"

"It's an isolation tank. It's supposed to be minimally accessible to give the feeling—" Hana began, but Vivian's look of quick anger silenced her.

"Should one of us just….go in there?" Gael asked. The question that all of us hadn't wanted to voice.

158

Vivian let out a long huff of air. "As the captain, it should be me."

"No," I said, and startled myself. "I'm the one with the most extensive water training."

And it was true. Though everyone trained in an NBL, I'd done a longer, more advanced course. I could hold my breath for almost three minutes underwater, could swim the length of a giant pool, back and forth, until my arms felt like they'd float away from me if I didn't pin them down. None of the others could disagree with me, though I could see that all of them were fighting a dueling feeling of wanting to disagree with me and also being glad that they wouldn't have to go in the tank.

"It still should be me," Vivian said.

"It's going to be me," I said.

There were tank suits along the wall, and I suited up quickly. The rush before the dive came back to me. How I used to love the feeling of my suit as it snugged against my skin. I replaced my flash beam around my wrist.

"Just look around quick. Don't go diving under the water if you don't see anything. We're not a rescue squad. Just do your due diligence." Alec said.

I climbed up the tank and swung my legs around the hatch, feeling them dangle in the air. There was a short drop, just one or two feet into the water. I whispered, "Roll," and then I let myself go.

22

When they got me out of the pool, I was in such shock that my body couldn't stop thrashing around. Someone injected a sedative, and I dropped into the darkness of induced sleep.

Even years later, I remembered the dream I'd had. I was home, at my mother's house, out in the country. We had this long, winding dirt road, and I used to walk it every day to get the mail while I was growing up. In the dream, I was doing the walk, and my mother walked next to me. She was pointing out different kinds of prairie flowers that grew alongside the road. "That's Queen Anne's Lace, you can eat it, you know. But you have to be careful, it doesn't look that far from hemlock."

She reached down and picked the flower, its large white head a cluster of tiny flowers. She handed it to me and I held it to my face, trying to inhale the smell. I noticed tiny black ants crawling across it, then. They scattered in patterns, moving out concentrically. "Look, they're making a galaxy," I said.

But my mother was no longer there.

19

In the isolation tank, I couldn't see anything at first. The water was slightly warm, pleasant even. But the darkness, even with both hatches open, was heavy around me. I switched on my flash beam and saw a body floating, face down, not far from me. I didn't let the panic take me. Not this time. I moved toward the body and moved it enough to see that the person was well past saving.

"Hello?" I shouted into the darkness.

Below me, I saw lights. At first, I thought it was the reflection from my flash beam. But it came from under the water, a glowing more than a shine of light. My mind flashed back to the eel's eyes. It was the same kind of flicker and shimmer.

Something brushed past me, another body floating. The lights were rising beneath me. I wouldn't panic. It wasn't really there. I had to keep telling myself that.

16

Gage was the first person I saw when I woke up. He was sitting next to me, as I lay in a medroom bed. I turned to him and tried to say something, but my tongue felt thick and useless in my mouth.

He held a glass of water out, straw pointing towards me, and I slurped at it. "It's those knockout meds, they dry your mouth out."

"How'd I get out? What was that thing?" I croaked out.

"You panicked. It could've happened to any of us. Seeing Dev like that. You panicked. You were rising too fast."

He filled me in on almost everything, though everything would come later when they thought I could handle it better. When we'd found Sidonie, I'd freaked out, undone my weights, and begun a panic swim in what I thought was upwards but wasn't. Several of the others had had to come to my rescue, bring me back up.

Dev had been working on fixing one of the lights when a piece of the replica sprang up. Under any normal circumstance, the glass on his helmet would have taken the hit fine, but he and Sidonie had been trying to modify his mask, between dives, to see better under the water—a mod that they hadn't discussed with anyone and which weakened areas of the mask. When the piece sprang up, it had smashed the mask with ease. Sidonie had panicked, hyperventilating until she passed out in her suit. It was a miracle she'd survived, though she'd never swim again.

"What did you see under there?" Gage asked.

"A….I don't know a fish or monster…or…" I let out a laugh. "And I saw that damn strand of Tenley's hair."

Gage's eyes widened just slightly, but enough that I knew he hadn't told me something.

"What?" I asked, but I knew.

12

The lights got closer. I wasn't going to give in to them, give in to the fear I felt crawling up under my skin, scrunching its way across my bones.

"Hello?" I shouted into the darkness.

And the darkness answered, "Help."

A tiny voice to my left. I moved through the water towards it. Something beneath me brushed my leg. Not human, something sinuous and water-slithering. I kept moving towards where I'd heard the voice. Below me, I could see that the lights were next to me, circling me.

"Help," the voice but slightly louder. I reached out and found a hand. Her skin was cold, but she grasped my fingers. I pulled the woman to me. "Don't let them touch you too much," she whispered into my ear.

Again, it brushed against me, circling my leg. I kicked out my legs, and I saw the lights scatter away. I began to swim, one arm around the woman, back towards the hatch. "Help!" I yelled it out, hoping my crew would hear me.

Beneath me, the lights got closer, and I could see there were bodies everywhere in the water. Hair brushed against my hand. I thought of blonde strands dangling in front of me.

9

The thing about sims is you're supposed to still follow protocol, make sure everyone is accounted for. The thing about sims, though, is that you're never really in danger, and so following protocol is easy.

In the rush to get Sidonie and me up to safety, no one noticed that Tenley wasn't among the people who reached the surface.

We watched her vid later. How she'd continued working on a section, her radio down, though no one knew. Her partner moved in front of her, then moved faster away from her, going towards the rescue efforts on the other side of the replica. Tenley began to go forward, and then she stopped, staring off into the depths of the pool for a few minutes. As if she saw something in the deep. Then she continued moving, but she'd stop every ten feet or so and look out for a bit. After almost 80 minutes of it, she'd finally just stopped. We watched the vid, and the way it stretched on forever without her moving. Even though I knew what had happened, knew the vid would stay in that spot as long as her battery lasted, I still willed her to move on.

They weren't sure exactly what happened. Some malfunction in the equipment that told her the wrong amount of time left, her own foggy misreading of it, but she should have had enough warning to have started the ascension soon enough to have survived.

I watched the vid later, alone, trying to see what had kept her staring off into the depths. But all I saw were shadows.

5

It was Hana who reached down and pulled the woman to safety. Then Alec helped me out. He stared into the water, "What the hell are those lights?"

We all peered down into the tank at them, swimming just below the surface, eyes up to stare at us.

The woman babbled out a few words, but we couldn't make sense of them. Later, we'd learn that it was some kind of experiment. Nothing was ever told to us conclusively, just that they'd been testing a fish in the tank with people for some kind of therapy. We weren't given the reason, just that people started getting obsessed with going into the tank. Eventually, they all went in, and only one came back out.

3

I visited the woman some months later, but she was restricted in what she could legally say. We talked around the subject, but she asked me something as I was getting up to leave.

"You were in that NBL sim that went wrong, right?"

I nodded.

"I thought so. You get it, then, what it's like to be in the dark, in that water."

"Yeah," I said.

She sighed. "It makes you feel so safe, right up until you drown."

"Don't carry the weight of surviving with you," I said. "It weighs on you more than that water."

"What else am I supposed to carry?" she responded.

I didn't have a good answer, and so I left.

1

Some nights, I go to the local swimming pool, and the night guard lets me in because he likes me. I float on my back and stare at the sky. In the dark, floating in the water, I can almost think that I'm in the stars. Right when I feel like I'm about to fly, I let myself sink.

Like the Absence

Fifteen years later, on the bus, I ran into a girl who'd been in our grade. I didn't recognize her, and still can't say what her name was, though I'm sure she told it to me in the slew of words that she rushed out about her husband and her three children and her two dogs and her job working at the local school. It was her job that led to the conversation about sixth grade.

"God, I still just shudder, actually shudder when I think about it, you know? To have been that close to tragedy. It makes me wonder how we all got through it. Such a thing at such a young age. It certainly made it worse that our school was so small; there was just no getting away from it."

I stared at her hard, trying to picture how she must have looked at age twelve, trying to pick out her face among the many blurred faces that sometimes infiltrated my dreams. I didn't remember her. Not at all. So I nodded along and hoped that she didn't really remember me either.

...

There were five of us: two boys and three girls. At the end of the school year, there'd be four of us.

I was the one with one foot already somewhere else. My parents had decided that we were moving after the school year ended. My father hated the town for as long as I could remember. We were going back to the city where my parents had met and which I romanticized. I never really let on how much I wanted out. Not to the others, at least, I never wanted to hurt anyone by letting them know that I would have given them all up in a second for skyscrapers.

I didn't believe in most things that people our age did. I never thought that I'd ever be special, and that made me content.

It was probably because of this unnerving practicality that they didn't tell me at first. They knew that my first reaction was going to be a sigh. I was also sick that week and, in elementary school, a week away was like ten years behind bars. A thousand things happened: friendships dissolved; gossip was spread, believed, recanted in tears, and then remolded to be spread again; teacher's pets were suddenly the last person you would have expected; new alliances were forged; and sometimes, on very rare occasions, lives changed for real without anyone realizing it.

...

In college, my junior year, after drunkenly rushed sex with a guy I met at a party, we were lying in his bed, and he told me a ghost story. Or he thought it was a ghost story.

"So, a friend of my brother's grew up like four, five hours north of here. This really little ho fucking hum town, you know the type where there's church, there's hunting, and there's a helluva lot of bars but there isn't anything else? Well, my brother's friend he's like three years younger than us. I guess this kid, who was a few years older, died at his school. Like on the school property, in front of a whole bunch of people. Fucked up, right? Well, it gets worse. This kid started being seen around the place. Hiding out in the playground equipment, going down the slide ahead of kids, laughing in the hallways. People swore on it. All covered in blood and grotesque looking."

"There wasn't any blood." I said it hushed, not really to him or anyone other than myself.

"What?" he asked.

I realized I was in bed, mostly naked, next to some guy who I didn't even know the name of except that it ended in the letter 'n'—John or Ben or Ryan. I disentangled myself from the sheets, found my pants, my top, not even bothering with my bra, and hurried into them as he asked me over and over if I was alright.

...

166

Lena was the quiet one. She never really spoke except to tell us when we were doing things wrong, so actually, she spoke a lot but had a tiny voice. A born leader who didn't have the power that she wanted. I always thought this was probably the reason for everything. That's being unfair to Lena, though. There was no way she could have wanted things to go as far as they did. Still, she was the first to say she saw the ghost.

...

"Lena, stop!" someone shrieked with delight, and even years later, I turned and expected to see her.

Just two girls, maybe thirteen or fourteen—at the age where they looked like the women they'd become eventually, but with none of the signs of aging, of the tiny losses that mark each passing year.

I watched them, for a moment, and imagined the alternate world where that was my teenage life. Where things hadn't broken apart.

...

Luke was the one who liked magic tricks. I always thought that was the only reason he was part of our group and not one of the jocks. He could run super fast and jump higher than anyone I'd ever known, but he didn't like sports because that kind of practice would take away from practicing his magic. He wanted to be Harry Houdini, but as he explained to us on more than one occasion, he wanted to be a Harry Houdini who was actually a good magician. None of us understood what he meant, but we'd nod along anyway.

He believed Lena immediately. Or at least that's how I heard it later, when I was back at school, still getting over the edge of my cough. He told me the story first, excited like I'd never seen anyone excited— practically jumping up and down as he told me.

"You have to believe me, oh my god, it's the best thing ever. Lena saw a ghost!"

There came my patented sigh.

"Just listen, it's true! She saw a ghost in the playground!"

"A ghost of who?" I asked, already mentally preparing my list of anti-ghost facts.

"A girl, a girl who died here!"

And there we had it. I knew that finding out if anyone had ever died at the school would be easy. I sighed again but, this time, in a different way. I liked to prove people wrong.

…

At my high school graduation, I looked out over the crowd of faces, and there was almost no one out there whom I knew. A big city meant a big graduating class. I knew maybe ten percent of the people in my grade. I liked even less of them and was friends with none. I'd once overheard some girls talking about me in the locker room, not realizing I was still in the shower and could hear them perfectly fine.

"She's just weird, so quiet, like she's afraid that if she speaks, she doesn't know what will come out of her mouth."

It made me think of the fairy tale where the two sisters are cursed. One with jewels that pour from her mouth for every word she speaks. One with snakes. I wasn't sure which I'd be, or if screams counted as words anyway.

"You know, I've never seen her talk to anyone unless if she's answering a question."

"Fucked up. You think she's got drug problems or something?"

I'd almost started laughing, barely containing the sound that wanted to burst from my chest, wishing that my quietness stemmed from drug problems.

…

Sharifa was the one we all wanted most to succeed. Smart and pretty, but also sadder than any of us could really understand at that age. I used to dream of her with bird wings. She'd spread them out and jump off things. The wings never worked. She was the one I most wanted to believe had really seen something.

We never went over to her house when we played. She said that her mother didn't like a lot of noise, though once, I overheard my parents discussing her family.

"That sister of hers, god, how could something like that happen?" my mother's voice.

"Did you ever see her father? I'm glad Marta doesn't go over there. The guy's got something wrong in him. I wouldn't doubt that he had something to do with it."

"David, Jesus, don't say something like that."

And then silence. I'd heard about Sharifa's sister. Little pieces of information. Her older sister had been found in a parking lot, murdered. She was eleven years older than us, and it happened when I was not even three yet. There wasn't much information, or not much that trickled down to my age group's ears. I thought about it years later. Not just the horror of the crime or the horror that must have hit that family, but, the horror of whoever found her, some small body lying in the middle of a parking lot, and upon finding her, the person must have known that there was no going back for this little girl, and that in finding her, there was no going back for them either.

"I believe Lena, Marta. Why can't you *ever* just believe us?" Sharifa asked me, her voice so annoyed.

She thought I was being mean. I thought I was just being me, having always believed that my part in this friendship was to be the voice of reason.

...

When I found out I was pregnant, I didn't believe it at first. The first pregnancy test flashed the little pink plus sign, and I dropped it, like something cursed, something I needed to have away from me.

Ten pregnancy kits later, convincing myself that some kind of variation on hysterical blindness was making me see a plus sign instead of a minus one, I finally gave in.

I was twenty-nine and had never wanted children. I especially didn't want a child like this, given the uncertainty of the father being overseas, a journalist covering the war. I didn't want to think that he wouldn't come back. Yet, somehow knowing that there was a baby, partly his, growing inside me, made it seem more likely that he wouldn't come back. Tragedy always strikes when it can affect the most people. That's what I came to believe. It's what I learned in the sixth grade.

...

Tom was the one who was my best friend, the first person I met in the first grade, and we stuck with each other after that. Smart and funny and with a smile that could win us out of any situation at school.

"Why didn't you tell me that they were all going crazy?" I asked him as we walked home.

"Every time I called, your mom said you were in bed. What did you have anyways? The chicken pox?"

"Just a cold." A lie. I had started feeling sick on a Sunday, and my parents thought I was faking to get out of school. By Monday, though, my fever spiked to 104, and I was delirious, screaming about how there was a woman in my room. I said she was scared and needed my help. My parents told me this later and asked if I remembered any of it. I didn't. They rushed me to the ER, where I was put on an IV. My fever came down, but kept returning, and every time it did, I started screaming and crying and begging for someone to just let me help her. I had to stay in the hospital for two days and then was bedridden, doctor's orders, for the rest of the week.

"I wish my parents would let me stay home for a week with just a cold." Even then, I think Tom could always tell when I wasn't being completely honest. But he never once pushed me into saying what I wasn't ready to tell.

...

At twenty-seven, I stepped out of a café, reading a newspaper headline, holding a hot coffee, and didn't look where I was going.

"Marta?" Someone said—voice hesitant, wondering.

I looked up, expecting to see someone I half-knew, but didn't like, from at work. Instead, it was a handsome guy I didn't recognize. Tall with dark hair and flashing green eyes. I still wouldn't have recognized him, but then he smiled. That smile was unforgettable.

"Tom?"

He smiled again, and then I was smiling too. I had never thought that I'd smile upon seeing one of them again. But there he was, and there I was.

He was heading somewhere, and I was heading somewhere, and so we made plans for later. We got dinner, and then dessert, and then coffee, and then drinks, and finally we ended up back at my place. I would have thought that we'd no longer have anything in common. We had both left our twelve-year-old selves so far behind us. Yet, we talked as if we had kept up over the years, as if our lives had always been running alongside each other, just waiting for the chance to meet back up. We talked for hours until we both finally fell asleep on my couch. I woke up aching and watched him sleep. He looked peaceful. I didn't think that I could ever look like that.

...

I looked up deaths in the town. Of young people. I wasn't sure what Lena's definition of a girl was, so I looked for anyone under twenty. There were several that might have fit the bill, but none happened at the school, or for that matter, anywhere near the school. I took this as my evidence.

"How do you know it was reported?" Lena asked.

"What? How are they not going to report on a story about a dead kid on school property? That has newspaper gold written all over it." Tom said, always in my corner.

"Tell her what the ghost told you, Lena, tell her!" Sharifa said, a note in her voice that I'd never heard before.

"The ghost said that we're all going to die."

"Oh, really?" I raised one eyebrow—the back-up gesture to my patented sigh of disdain.

Lena nodded solemnly.

Luke's eyes grew round and he gasped, "I didn't know that! You didn't tell me that! Why would the ghost say something like that?"

"She's trying to warn us," Sharifa said.

"Oh, whatever." That was me. I left.

Tom followed me out. "Why do people always want to believe in ghosts and then always make them out to be scary?"

I turned to him. "What do you mean?"

He shrugged. "Well, it's just, if I were to think that ghosts were real, were really real, well then I'd think of them as good signs, you know, signs that things do go on. I don't think they'd be here to scare us, they'd just want to let us know that things are okay."

"I don't believe in them," I said, but then thought about it for a second. "But, if I did, and I don't, I'd think they'd be ourselves that we were seeing. Like us, if things went differently, and they'd want us to get it right this time."

"You know, for believing in nothing, you always sound like you wish you did." Even then, Tom knew me better than anyone. I tried to raise my eyebrow at him, but all I could do was smile back.

...

When Tom kissed me, all those years later, I couldn't help but remember when he had said, in all seriousness at age eight, that one day we'd be married. By nine, he would deny this statement, saying I'd dreamed it, but I'd remembered clearly how happy the thought had made me that I could have Tom forever.

That night, I started crying. He just held me.

"Please, please, just tell me that we're going to be okay. That it's not going to come true."

He held me tighter but didn't say anything.

...

I had avoided them, expecting that they'd come to their senses any day and we'd be back to normal. They didn't. I finally cornered Luke one day to ask him what was going on.

"We can't talk to you and Tom anymore." He tried to say it with force, but it came out pleading.

"What? Why?"

"Because you don't believe."

"Do you? I mean, really, Luke?"

He shrugged. "I really want to. It's fun. Believing in stuff."

"That's a stupid reason."

"Sharifa really does. She's been talking to the ghost." His eyes grew a little big as he was saying this.

"Oh? Have you had a little convo with this ghost, as well?"

He looked down. "No."

"Uh-huh, well, when you do, then I'll believe." If there is one conversation in my life that I wish I could replay, it would be that one, even if I couldn't change what happened later. I would have wanted to change how I said it. I would have wanted to joke a little more. To make him laugh.

Lena sent me a note in class. It said simply: *The ghost says you and Tom still count.* I hadn't understood it, but I glared at her anyway.

...

He said he had to go. He didn't look me in the eye. I knew that they *have to go* came from his *want to go*. He was always going to be the one who was willing to go anywhere for that one good story.

"It's just a month or two. Then I'll be back. It'll be fine. I'll be fine."

"Did you ever look them up?" I asked, deciding it was my turn to be hurtful.

"Who?"

I stared at him.

"Oh. No. I haven't. I've thought about it. But I haven't."

"I did. I *did*."

"Don't tell me. Tell me when I get back. I'll be fine."

"Fuck you, Tom. They're both dead. And you're still going to leave me. Fuck you."

I didn't even say goodbye.

...

My parents never asked me why I was quieter that week. Why did only Tom come over? They must have thought I was still in recovery mode. I told him about the fevers then, about how I'd been delirious.

"But you don't remember?"

"Not really. It's like I can almost remember. I can remember the woman, sort of, she seemed familiar and like she needed me to tell her something. She kept touching her stomach and then touching me. I didn't know what to tell her." It was the most I'd remembered and only remembered it as I told him, like it was something that was only meant to be shared between the two of us.

It happened the next day. It seemed so normal to start with. Everything was going fine. Until it wasn't. Luke passed me in the hall, said we were all meeting up on the school roof. Said I could come along again. I told Tom.

174

I'd looked up Lena first. I was twenty, and my roommate was twenty-one. I drank more than I should have. There was really only the one article. Or only one that I needed. Lena had been nineteen, overdosed on heroin, and found by her boyfriend. In the picture they used for the article, she looked much older. There is something always strange about the photographs they run when people die, always picking that one picture that instantly makes you know the article isn't going to be happy. You don't even need to read the headline.

I sat shaking for hours, and my roommate came back and took one look at me. "Jesus, Marta, you really have a problem."

I stared at her, nodding. I had a problem.

...

We figured out how to get on the school's roof by the time we were in the fourth grade. A quick pick of a single, simple lock. Luke, of course, was good with locks.

The building was only two stories high. It was hardly dangerous to be up there. Tom and I found them all sitting around in a tiny circle.

"What's up?" I asked.

"The ghost told me again. She said that we're all going to die." Lena looked scared. For the first time, I doubted my doubt.

"But I have an idea," Sharifa said.

"An idea?" I asked. Tom touched my shoulder. He was looking at Luke. Luke was near tears.

"We just have to show the ghost that we're not afraid."

"Not afraid of dying? But aren't we?"

Sharifa glared at me. I wondered if her sadness had somehow changed, mutated to anger without any of us realizing. Or maybe that's only in retrospect that I recognize that. Maybe in that moment, I hadn't really gotten that at all.

"We just, just have to make it look like we're not afraid," Luke said.

I stared at him. Tom touched my arm again.

"It's like a magic trick," Sharifa said. "There isn't really any magic. But you still believe it. You still really think that something is happening. Something magical."

All three of them stood up, walking to the edge of the roof.

"What are you guys doing?" Tom asked.

"Magic." Sharifa smiled. I thought of my dreams, and then I thought of how I found her crying once in the girls' bathroom. She was sobbing and pulling her own hair. She said that she felt dirty and just wanted to stop. I had patted her shoulder, trying to console her. She had begged me not to tell anyone and, in keeping with the childish idea of honor, I hadn't.

I didn't think they were going to jump. Not really, but Tom must have because he covered my eyes. One of them screamed. I think it was Lena. I heard children screaming from the playground. But it was the cracking that really got to me. The sharpness of that crack.

It was just two stories up, and they should have been hurt, but okay. They all should have been basically alright. Tom and I ran down the steps; we ran outside. He was holding my hand. Sharifa was lying on the ground, howling in pain, clutching her leg. I could see bone sticking out. Lena seemed okay, shaken, cut, but okay. She was sobbing. It was Luke who, at first, I didn't notice. He was just lying there, staring at the sky. In that instant, I thought, of course Luke is the one who's not upset or hurt; he's the one who knows how to do magic tricks.

But the crowd around him drew closer, and I noticed how he wasn't moving; he wasn't just not getting up; he wasn't moving at all.

We were all counseled, everyone at the school, but especially the four of us. We were his friends—had seen him die. I corrected the therapist.

"I didn't really see him die. I saw him about to jump, and then I saw him dead. But I didn't see him die." I kept repeating this, over and over, because I wanted to believe it. I never could believe anything.

My parents moved earlier than we had expected. They didn't want me stuck with the memories. I said goodbye to no one. Not even Tom.

"Are you alright, sweetie?" my mother kept asking.

"I think I'm going to die." I kept saying. "The ghost said we were all going to die."

They thought I was delirious again.

. . .

I didn't need to look Sharifa up. At twenty-five, I saw the story on the news. A young woman who killed herself, jumping off a twenty-story building while wearing a homemade set of angel wings. The wings didn't work. I almost didn't need to see the name to know who it was.

That left two of us. I didn't look Tom up because I couldn't stand the thought that it was only one of us. When we found each other again, I tried to believe that I still didn't believe.

The doctor confirmed my pregnancy with a smile. "Would you like to call your husband?"

"He's overseas. It's the wrong time of day there."

"I think he'd be willing to be woken up for this." Again, a smile.

I tried to smile back.

At home, I called Tom's number. It rang and rang and rang. The news about the bombing was the top story of the night. Twelve people killed, two of them American journalists, thirteen others injured. I touched my stomach, imagining that I could feel the heartbeat, so small and strange and alive inside of me.

"Please help me," I said it out loud, to no one.

I touched my stomach, trying to let the baby know that I was still there, trying to be alright. I thought I heard someone screaming that she needed to help me.

I fell asleep somewhere in there and had a dream that I was standing on the roof of our old school. Luke, Lena, and Sharifa were all there. They looked older—all the same age as me. Luke was wearing a suit, the one he was buried in. It fit him well. He was shuffling a deck of cards. He held them out to me, and I took one. It was the ace of spades. He took it back from me to throw it over the roof's edge. It turned into a bird, as it fell, and flew away.

"That's really good, Luke!"

He shrugged, "Things get easier to do the more you practice at them."

Lena laughed at that. She was in a red dress, looking beautiful. I forgot how much I liked her laugh. Her laugh wasn't quiet. It was loud and could fill up rooms.

Sharifa was in blue. She seemed happier, smiling at me. "It's beautiful here, isn't it?"

And it was, the trees went on forever, and the roof was filled with seashells, and the sky was the perfect summery shade.

"Where's Tom?" I asked.

Luke shook his head. "Not yet. There's someone here who wants to speak to you."

It was then I noticed the girl. She was maybe fourteen or so. I think I always knew that. She was lovely, like everything all at once.

She smiled. "I'm sorry. Sometimes what we're saying gets mixed up, lost along the way."

"What do you mean?"

"I just, I just wanted to make it easier on her." She looked at Sharifa. I knew. "I wanted to tell her, you know?"

"What?"

"I wanted to tell her that everyone has to die, but that it's okay. You shouldn't be scared. It's okay."

Everything over a message that was supposed to make things better. Tom, always almost right about everything.

"But, it's so hard before that."

She nodded. "Can I do something for you?"

"What do you mean?"

"Will you believe in something for just a second?"

"But, what?"

"Believe that when you were a little girl, you saw the future and you didn't like how it looked. But you forgot. You forgot, and you ended up doing things just like you knew you shouldn't. Because you were in love and you'd seen a thousand bad things happen and you just wanted one person to have forever. And what you never understood is that in believing in him, you were believing, and that's what mattered, and the future wasn't what you thought. Not everything is what you see. The messages get garbled. We mess them up."

"But, I don't…"

"When you were a little girl, you wanted to help her, more than anything, but you couldn't, you were sick. Tell her that everything's going to be okay. And believe it. Really believe it."

I looked at Luke, Lena, and Sharifa. They all looked so beautiful. I thought, what if everyone was always trying to help, but they just messed things up? A little girl mishears a message, a little boy practices magic and thinks he can help, another little girl just wants to get away.

I woke up, clutching my stomach, sobbing. Standing over me was me. Twelve years old and covered in fever sweat. I couldn't help her, couldn't go back in time and make things better. I touched my stomach and then touched her, wanting to give her some sense of peace. To know that one day there might be something that would make all this okay. Even if that something was a heartbeat, tiny and imperceptible, but beating, nonetheless. She vanished as the phone rang.

I picked it up.

"Hello?"

"Hey, it's me. I'm fine. It's okay. I wasn't there."

And in that moment, I believed.

Bring Out Your Dead, We've Been Waiting to Talk to Them

My lover's last thoughts were of a game he'd played as a kid. There were trees and hiding, and the sun dipping low on the horizon. When RE:Memory first came out, everyone thought it would provide closure. There was something comforting about the idea of seeing your loved ones' last thoughts displayed in front of you—the images that played through their heads as everything else emptied out. The problem is that no one considered what it would be like to watch your loved ones' last thoughts and not find yourself in there.

RE:Memory was hailed as one of the most exciting innovations in the future of death—at last, a way to understand the ones you'd lost. Everyone got on board, having an RE:Memory sensor attached—a simple outpatient procedure. It recorded all of your thoughts in 5-minute loops, erased as they went on. That way, if you died unexpectedly, and what deaths weren't unexpected, you'd have the final 5 minutes. "We don't sacrifice your privacy," the commercials said, as a woman smiled into the camera as she snuck into an early morning spa retreat from work. "All data, save for the last five minutes of your life, is erased continuously."

David said he wasn't interested. "It's like letting a spy into your house, while fully knowing they're a spy." But I liked the thought of having some tangible proof after death that a life had been lived. The software worked by capturing the last thoughts as the brain flickered, after the body was gone, those synapses firing off into nothingness. That way, you didn't have to see the fear or pain; there was just whatever the mind went to as it ended. My favorite of the commercials featured an older man dying in a hospice as his children race to get there on time. They don't make it before he's gone, but the RE:Memory video plays and shows him remembering a birthday party the year before, where all of his family was gathered around him. The man's children embrace at the end of the ad, as RE:Memory's tagline, "We'll tell them goodbye for you," flashed across the screen.

I got the RE:Memory first, and it was only through persistence that David finally agreed. He did it for me. "You'll watch mine, right, if I die first?" I asked him one night, as we were tucked into each other's bodies. "I don't want to do that," he said. "Why?" He shrugged, the slight move of his shoulders against my chest reminded me of all the times he'd hug me from behind when I was in the kitchen or at my desk. "It feels like something we're not supposed to know. Questions that shouldn't be answered until we meet up again in some other place." I left it at that. I'd never believed in an afterlife, imagined that the ground was everything we had to look forward to, and so wasn't one last glimpse of knowledge something we deserved to have?

I first started hearing complaints through the grapevine at work. A secretary's sister had died in a car accident. Her RE:Memory was a memory of getting her cat. The secretary said, "I practically raised her, and she just thinks about Mr. Tibbles?" I brushed it away, thinking about how our animals were often like family to us, and so it made sense that they'd take up our thoughts as well. David sent me an article about how people were complaining because some RE:Memories seemed nonsensical: last thoughts about impossible cities that the person had dreamed about, just flashes of colors, songs stuck in their heads on the day they died.

Some people had started asking for their money back from RE:Memory, and spouses discussed a class-action lawsuit, saying RE:Memory was sending fraudulent memories in place of the real ones. One woman being interviewed said, "There's no way my wife wasn't thinking about me. There's no way." The woman's voice sounded like cutting out phone signals, like the sound of trees falling, like she'd never climb back up to life if she couldn't be angry about this.

RE:Memory's legal team pointed out the minutiae of the contracts that were signed when someone used their software. They also addressed the fraudulent claims by simply asking, "What would be the point of that?" No one had an answer.

David said, "I told you this wasn't a great idea," over dinner. He ladled pasta onto my plate, and his hip brushed against me as he walked past. "Maybe," I said, but I didn't believe myself. I still thought it was something good in the face of something terrible.

And then, not long after, David died. A simple thing—just a clot that was never suspected. The doctors told me, "He wouldn't have felt much. It would have been quick." I barely heard them, but maybe we never hear them and they're saying it more for themselves—because they needed to say something.

I watched his RE:Memory alone, at home, in the bed that now felt like it stretched out and out in emptiness. Why had we gotten such a big bed?

On the screen, there was a forest. His childhood friends were running in front of him. They were laughing and shrieking with joy. He was the one chasing them. It was tag or some iteration of it. All those games we made up as children were all simulations of the life we'd have as adults: the looking and the running away.

The sun dipped down behind the trees. I was nowhere in the memory. Just this childhood game, and him running forward. He shouted, "I'm gonna find you!" and the RE:Memory went to darkness.

Tethering

When the waves move around her, Kari imagines outer space. The rush and roll of weightlessness. She hears her mother's voice from so far away that it could be galaxies. It could be lifetimes. Everyone was here once. Everyone is here, she thinks.

But that comes both earlier and later. At 41, Kari lives in a state surrounded by water that she never goes into. Her wife was almost in the Olympics once, as a diver, and tries to coax her out into the waves whenever she can, but Kari puts out a blanket on the beach and reads instead. Kari likes being close to the water, close enough to hear it, without going into it—like exposure therapy if the goal was to never get cured, to know that you had the power. Some days, she even goes when Louise doesn't. On her days off, she catches up on reading before doing chores. If she hears a child yell too loud, though, enough to break the trance of whatever book she is inside of, Kari will jolt out of her skin for a moment.

But it was an actual scream. Kari dropped her book and scanned the beach for who made the sound. Almost no one was there, just a girl, maybe twelve or thirteen, pointing at the water and screaming. Kari's gaze went to the waves, and she remembered seeing a child in the water when she first started reading. A little boy in bright blue swim trunks. But she can't see him now, and the girl is still screaming.

Wait, Kari thinks. Wait.

"Kar, can you grab me the oats?" Louise is rubbing sugar and butter together between her fingertips, creating the coarse sandiness of a crumble topping. They've only just moved back to Louise's home, Kari's hesitance finally giving way to Louise's longing, and the kitchen isn't yet set up how either of them would like it.

Kari opened the cupboard and moved a few jars around before locating the oats. Reaching for them for a moment, she remembered all the times she'd reached for a jar of oats, sitting on the counter, helping her mom. She handed them to Louise. "What are you making?"

"A pineapple crumble."

"That sounds lovely," Kari says. She stares at the light dancing through the window. She'll need time to get used to the light here.

"What are you thinking about?" Louise asks, always able to catch the moments when Kari is hovering outside herself.

Kari rarely speaks about her mother to Louise, holding the memories tight to her, so instead she says, "Have you ever seen a ghost?"

Louise stops what she's doing, chuckles, "Interesting train of thought. I don't think so?"

"You'd think you'd know for sure, right? If you saw a ghost? It'd be such a life-changing event that it'd be concrete, firm, striking."

Louise shrugged, "No, I think you'd always question it. Or it might happen, and you wouldn't be sure if it were a coincidence or something real, something tangible. Maybe we deal with ghosts all the time. A dream, a person who reminds you of someone you loved, an almost accident that you correct at the last chance."

Kari thinks about it. A life laid out behind her in tiny moments. "Did I ever tell you about Oatmeal cream pies?"

Kari's mother never cooks or bakes much; her shifts at the hospital always keep her longer than she hopes, so she prefers the quick instant rice and a bag of veggies, a burrito from the restaurant across the street, anything filling and at least vaguely nutritious. But at least once a month, she bakes oatmeal cream pies. Her grandmother used to make them for her mother on sick days, and her mother did it for her, and now she does it for Kari when they can spend a few hours together, uninterrupted by her work or Kari's school. Oatmeal cookies made extra big, soft, chewy enough to have some bend to support the sandwich filling. Just a little heat of cinnamon. The center is fluffy vanilla buttercream spread thick enough to squeeze out when you take a bite.

Even as a small child, Kari never liked things to be too sweet, but the one exception was always these cookies. When she is very tiny, she perches on the counter like a sprite, and then as she grows, she sits, legs dangling. Grabbing things from the cupboards as her mom asks for them. A jar of oats, the red rust of the cinnamon in the air as her mom poured it out, the sound of the old electric beater chugging along through the thick dough.

The last time they make cookies together, Kari is thirteen and her mother asks her if she remembers her dreams when she wakes up. Kari has to think about it, really think about it, if she remembers them or just the feelings they leave her with in the morning.

"Do you, Mom?"

"Not as much as I used to. I used to dream in such big colors," her mom says.

And when the call comes only a month later, while Kari is working on an essay for history class and her aunt is downstairs, it is Kari who answers. Though later, she convinces herself that it was her aunt who answered, her aunt who broke the news to her, instead of her to her aunt when she walks up to her in the kitchen and falls into her arms. Her aunt is not sure what has happened. She says, "Sweety, what is it? What is it?"

What is it? Kari wants to wait. Wait here.

Memory is a trick like that. How it shifts and shimmers before crushing us like a wave. Kari on the shore, gasping for breath, Kari underwater, Kari waiting. She waits.

Kari is twenty-three, working at the cafe in her college town the summer after graduation. She doesn't want a real job, yet, she tells her aunt on their weekly calls. She likes the regulars who come in every day, likes the chitchat, likes the sound of steam and coffee beans grinding, and though years later she'll realize the edges of hearing she's lost because of it, she never begrudges that time.

The girl comes in often, tries a different bakery item every time she does, and always gets a latte. She's fourteen or fifteen, Kari's never been great with guessing ages.

"Trying to pick a favorite?" Kari asks when the girl selects yet another different bakery item to go with her latte.

"I like food, trying to taste everything I can," the girl says. And in such a solemn way that it makes Kari laugh.

"You're on a mission!"

The girl smiles, as if she's pleased with the truth of Kari's statement. "What's your favorite?"

"Not much of a sweet fan, to be honest."

The girl keeps staring at her, the big smile tugging at her lips. "But, you still have a favorite? Everyone always still has a favorite."

Kari smiles back, the girl's sweetness a contagion. "Well, if I had to pick, I've always loved oatmeal creme pies."

"Not the store-bought?" The girl asks, incredulous and playfully aghast.

Kari plays along. "Never! Homemade. Only homemade."

Kari turning under the water. Her body so small that the waves are an elephant on top of her. She can't break through. But she can see red. No not red, not quite. Pink red. The color of hibiscus. Look at me all dressed in flowers, her mom had said when she showed her the swimsuit she'd pick out for herself, spinning around. Mom, you're gorgeous, Kari had exclaimed. And she'd meant it, she'd seen in that spin all of her mother's beauty unfold before her. How she must have looked young, before a husband who left, before her daughter, before a job that tired her out more than it did anything else. She was so beautiful. Hibiscus. Kari reaches out under the water.

"I wish I had met your mother," Louise said on their fifth date. "She sounds lovely."

"She was. She saved my life." Kari saw Louise's expression, realized that Louise had taken this metaphorically. She is nodding sagely as if to say, *Don't our mothers save us all?* "Like literally."

Louise's nod faltered. "Literally?"

"I was drowning once. We were on vacation. And I was drowning, and she rushed through the water, like she was a wave herself, and she saved me. I wasn't breathing by the time she got me to the shore, but there was a lifeguard, and he did CPR, I guess. I don't remember. But my mom was the one who saved me. Not him. She pulled me out of the water."

"Whoa. That must have been terrifying."

"I don't swim now, for sure," Kari said.

"Oh, of course, for you, but," Louise said. "I meant for your mom. My god, can you imagine?"

Wait. Time is a trick. It confuses and tears apart memory from the inside. Kari remembers her mom crying with joy when she sputtered out the water from her mouth as the lifeguard wrapped a towel around her shoulders. Her mother wept through a smile. "You're fine," she said. What a word—one syllable to contain a life.

The little girl pointed frantically, and Kari saw a flash of bright blue below the waves. She scanned the beach, looking for anyone. But everyone was too far away. If she were thinking, she'd remember that inexperienced swimmers were more likely to drown themselves than save someone drowning. That someone who isn't prepared can easily be dragged underwater by the startling weight of someone panicking as they take water into their lungs. But she had no time. There was no thinking.

Please, Kari thought. Wait. Wait.

"Wait," Kari says to her mom's boss on the phone. He is crying. "Wait. Please. I can't understand you."

"Wait, so what about the creme pies?" Louise asked. "What happened next?"

They were sitting at the counter. The pineapple crumble baking in the oven, the scent of cinnamon and sweet filling the air. Louise leaning forward, expectantly, waiting on Kari's story.

Her Saturday shift, and the girl walked in, all smiles. She came straight to the counter, a tote bag hanging off one arm. "I made you something!"

"You made me something. You might not understand how cafes work," Kari said.

The girl laughed. "It's a gift. I was thinking about your oatmeal creme pies." She reached into her bag and pulled out a Tupperware container with a purple lid. She set it on the counter. Kari looked at it, and the girl looked at her. Kari popped the lid open, and the scent was so startlingly familiar that she actually took a step back. The sandwiched cookies were stacked next to one another, golden colored oatmeal cookies with slightly darker, crispy edges. The cream right up to the edge.

"Thank you," Kari said. But she wasn't sure if she meant it.

"You're welcome," the girl said. And she meant it. "I—I hope you like them."

Kari tried to return to herself. "I'm sure I will. Really. It was very thoughtful."

The girl nodded once. "Okay, bye."

The air suddenly awkward, she turned around and left the cafe before Kari could say anything more. She closed the lid on the container and set it into her satchel. She forgot about it as the cafe's business picked up. Her regulars drifted in, joking, making orders that Kari could make in her sleep.

At home, that night, she'd gone to her satchel for her notebook, and instead found the container, the lid cracked slightly open in the shuffling of her walk home. She could smell her childhood kitchen. She popped it open. Pulled out one of the cookies and took a bite.

"I used to dream in such big colors," her mom says. "What's your favorite dream you ever had?" Kari asks.

"Oh, gosh, hmm." Her mom takes a thoughtful bite of her cookie. "When I was little, younger than you, I think, I used to have this dream that I could fly. I'd run along the bluff behind my parents' house. You know that big one at Grandma's?"

Kari nods. It was her favorite spot in all the world. She could see the town from the bluff, could hide in the sumac bushes and watch bees buzz in an out.

"Well, that was the bluff. I'd run and run and reach the edge, and in the dream I'd always be scared, but just for a second, and then I'd run right off the edge. But I didn't fall, I flew. I soared all over the town, circling all the houses."

Memory shook and shimmered when you weren't looking directly at it, changed and recreated.

"But this wasn't a memory. I was back there. I felt it so strongly. I was in the kitchen, talking to my mom, and eating those cookies. I've never, not ever, had something trigger a memory like that. That girl didn't make oatmeal cream pies. She made them exactly like my mom did. I can't explain it."

"But did you see the girl again? Did she come back?"

Kari shook her head. "I always wanted to thank her, like really thank her."

"Do you think she was a ghost?"

Kari in the water. Her mom pulling her to the surface. Kari is in the water, wrapping her arms around the little boy. She's trying. She's trying.

Cinnamon. Sweet. Browning butter. Red dust in the air. Not red pink. Hibiscus. Water. Sun. Turning, turning.

Kari drops the boy into the sand, her arms and legs shaking. His sister is crying. A few people have arrived, looking scared. A man steps forward, "I'm CPR certified."

But the boy is fine. He's coughing and scared. But he never drowned, just a second under, a moment when he couldn't tell if he was seeing the sand or the sky as he tossed and turned under the water. He looks up at Kari. "I'm fine!"

And what a word. It contained the universe.

Acknowledgments

Grateful to the editors of the following publications.

Astrolabe. "Alley Oop."
Cape Cod Poetry Review. "Other Vertigos."
Drunk Monkeys. "Someone Else's Sleeper."
Full of Crow. "All of Your Others."
Middle House Review. "Symbiosis."
Reckon Review. "Boy and Cave and Man and Night."
Rosebud. "A Sound Past Breaking."
Ruby. "Stone Fruit."
Sequestrum. "Under the Surface, Under the Light."
Short Story Long. "The Rushing Waves."
Supernatural Tales. "A Knocking Almost Like Hands," "Leopard Seals," and "Like the Absence."
The Wild Hunt. "A Path of Needles."

Nightmare Diaries. Moonstruck Books (2024). "In the Dark, They Say You Can't See What's Coming for You."

JackLeg Press Authors

jacklegpress.org

V. Joshua Adams
Mark Baumgartner
Gayle Brandeis
Scott Shibuya Brown
Michael Chin
Chloe Clark
Rivka Clifton
Brittney Corrigan
Jessica Cuello
Barbara Cully
Allison Cundiff
Curious Theatre Branch
Neil de la Flor
Genevieve DeGuzman
Suzanne Frischkorn
Victoria Garza
Reginald Gibbons
Joachim Glage
Caroline Goodwin
Brett Hanley
Summer Hart
Kathryn Kruse

Brigitte Lewis
Jenny Magnus
DK McCutchen
Jean McGarry
Rita Mookerjee
Mamie Morgan
Beau O'Reilly
Lex Orgera
Zach Powers
Karen Rigby
Jo Salas
Maureen Seaton
Kristine Snodgrass
Cornelia Spelman
Peter Stenson
Melissa Studdard
Jennifer Tseng
Gemini Wahhaj
Megan Weiler
David Welch
Cassandra Whitaker
David Wesley Williams